SHEENA CUNDY

The Madness and the Magic

a Witch Lit novel

For Mr. C
and a bright future.

Imperfection is beauty,
madness is genius, and it's better to
be absolutely ridiculous than absolutely
boring.

MARILYN MONROE

Contents

Acknowledgement

Gratitude to the Indie Author community and all its magic which helped to create this second edition of a debut novel.

1

Nasties and Neddies

C rafty Cottage waited in darkness at the end of the path. The row of orange faces beamed a glowing welcome at the children as they crept past. The four excited youngsters made slow, tentative steps to avoid the crooked smiles, stifling their giggles beneath silky black capes and long, white sheets. Stopping at the front door, the children glanced nervously at each other while the smallest child gasped at a bulbous-eyed monster staring at them from the porch.

'It's all right, Bill, it's only one of them gargoyle things…won't hurt ya,' said the oldest girl, pulling the small boy closer to her.

A thick wad of white, stringy web hung across one corner of the small porch, a large spider dangling in its midst.

'That's not a real cobweb!' blurted out Bill from the safety of his sister's side. 'You can tell it's not!'

'Shhh… Quiet now, or we won't get no sweets,' said another child as she held up her plastic pumpkin bowl by its handle and dangled it in front of Bill's face.

'Who's Sam?' asked an older boy, peering at a wooden plaque hanging on the door. 'It says… 'S-a-m-h-a-i-n greetings'.

What's that, then?' He turned to Bill's sister.

'I dunno…'

'And look,' he said, pointing underneath, "Happy New Year'?
It's only October…that's weird, innit?'

'Can we go?' Bill pleaded with his sister. She knew how
he hated the dark and, apart from the pumpkins, there was
no other lighting. Pressing her fingers hard to her lips at
the whimpering Bill, she reached across to the knobbly, brass
doorknocker…an owl, of all things.

Hesitating, she knocked twice in quick succession, wanting
to get it over with. This Halloween lark was becoming a bit
tedious. 'Honestly, anyone would think a Witch lived here or
something stupid,' she said, peering at the old fashioned broom
leaning against the gargoyle.

An empty silence fell on the children as they huddled close
and waited in the blackness, all eyes on the knobbly owl and
hearts pumping overtime. At first, they saw only a dim light
through the heavily frosted glass. But, as the door creaked
open and the gap widened slowly, they heard it…the croaking
voice of an old woman, singing: 'Trick or treat, I feel sick…' a
stooping figure appeared behind a candle. 'Hurry up and make
it quick…'

The eerie light flickered around her face.

'Don't around *my* door you dwell…else I will cast a nasty
spell!' She spat the words at the blackened faces and wide eyes.

Bemused expressions came over the older children's faces
and they managed a nervous laugh. It was all too much for Bill,
especially when the bent-up old woman emerged; lit by the
torch she was holding under her chin. The green, waxy skin
and hooked nose were a hideous sight. He cowered behind his
sister and fought back tears. The woman seemed to stand and

2

stare at him for hours before letting out a loud cackle.

'Well, well, well…what have we here? A Witch-fearing vampire! Wonders will never cease! Fear not, little one, I have a secret… I'm actually quite tame. In fact, my wickedness was taken from me almost three hundred years ago. Shall I tell you why?' Her voice softened. '*Apparently*, I showed an unusual tendency for liking children.' She smiled a toothless grin at him as a black spider bobbed from the rim of her bent and twisted hat, then turned to go back indoors.

'Can't think why. Must've been all those sweets I used to give them.'

Bill caught his sister flashing one of her big smiles at him as the Witch disappeared for a moment and returned with a black cauldron. It was a real one, he was sure of it.

'Here you are then,' she said. 'Some treats for your nerves, me dears.'

Reaching into the pot, she pulled out handful after handful of sweets and dropped them into their outstretched bowls and bags. The children swapped gleeful glances and thanked her before scurrying back down the path of orange faces.

'Don't eat them all at once,' she called after them. 'You'll spoil the magic!'

Bill looked round at the stooping old woman and shouted back, '*Sweets* aren't magic!'

'Now *that* is where you're wrong, because *everything* is magic, my dear young vampire…everything. Suck 'em and see!'

She cackled after them and disappeared inside.

'I don't believe that,' said Bill, stuffing a white chocolate mouse into his mouth and chewing it slowly.

'No of course you don't.' His sister herded him out on to the pavement and pulled him along by his cape. 'It's all just a bit of fun and there are no Witches anyway…she was only pretending!'

'I know that,' spluttered Bill. 'Can we go home now?'

* * *

Minerva smiled to herself as she leaned back against the front door. How entertaining! Another poor mite scarred for life, no doubt – but really, what did these children expect? All far too wrapped up in cotton wool nowadays; nothing like a good fright to wake them all up. And no better time for a little ghoulishness than Halloween. If she couldn't exploit her witchiness at this time of year, then when could she?

Her Pagan ways were as natural as breathing and to keep silent was harder than to dare.

The heavy long tresses of wig came away with the hat as she pulled it off and placed it on the hat stand in the hall. It was getting a bit hot under there.

'Until further *frighting* is required,' she said to the hairy hat. 'Time for a celebratory tipple, methinks, before the next bunch of tricksters arrive.' The brandy slipped down nice and easy between a miniature chocolate pumpkin or two. It was taste-bud heaven.

The thing about Minerva was that she lacked a certain amount of self-control, especially as far as brandy and choco-late were concerned. These delights, when added to a fine and worthy cause for celebration left no room for sobriety on that particular night. In fact, it wasn't long before she was well into her stride and dancing around the living room to a fast and furious Irish fiddle, blaring from the stereo. She soon picked up momentum, spurred on by the high energy as it filled her head with all kinds of images...

She was a Goddess, whirling and twirling in a ball of fire... She was a flame, dancing between the worlds... She was a soul, spinning around the cosmos... She was getting dizzy, and so caught up in the music, she didn't hear the doorbell go and continued in her chocolate and brandy-fuelled oblivion. Only when a dull thud on the living room window broke through the sound did she finally stop to look...and gasped.

'Whatever is *that*?' Minerva screamed at the window. A white, ghoulish face with blackened eyes and a bloody scar running down one cheek stared back at her. She had no idea who it was. Then it moved and she sensed a faint glimmer of recognition. It was the hair that did it, wobbling at a strangely familiar and crooked angle. She'd know that hair-piece anywhere.

A figure emerged to accompany the face as Minerva slid back the French window to find her friend on the patio. Isis was not in her usual attire of bright silks and satins, but was instead wearing a rather sinister-looking outfit of a white lab coat, dirtied with blood stains. What looked like half of an amputated arm hung lifelessly at one side. Now that she was in full view, Minerva could see the wonky hair-piece resting upon a bloody dagger through the head. Isis, in full, gory splendour, was a sight to behold. She wasn't sure whether to laugh or scream again and, managing neither, she stepped back to let her in.

'Isis...what the *hell* are you doing?'

'What does it look like I'm doing, Minerva? Do I need to state the obvious?'

'Well, I can see the *state* you're in. Quite clearly, you've had a costume change... Not exactly your usual look, is it?'

Isis spotted the brandy bottle on the table. 'Typical!' She puffed out the words in exasperation. 'You don't remember, do you? We were supposed to be *doing something* tonight... Really, Minerva, you are the absolute limit sometimes...and I've gone to all this *trouble!*'

Minerva was confused. 'You'll have to remind me, Isis,' she said, following her friend's gaze to the table. 'Care for a crafty tipple?'

Isis sighed, 'Oh, go on, then...'

Minerva made a quick exit to the kitchen and reappeared with a glass in her hand. Isis pointed at Minerva's head. 'Clearly I am not the only one dressed like this. You're not looking so hot yourself!'

The mere mention of the word was enough to send Minerva into one of her flushes and she began to fan herself like a nervous Geisha girl with the nearest Samhain card she could find.

'Well no... I mean yes, *hot* is exactly what I am! I suppose the dancing had something to do with it, but...' She cast her eyes upwards, to where her hooked green nose was strapped to the side of her head like a silly party hat. 'Oh *that*, yes...thought I'd have a little fun with the kiddies. Think it did the trick. It *was* on the right way round at the time.'

'You mean they laughed?' Isis spluttered into her drink.

'Not quite. But *I* did! It doesn't hurt to enter into the spirit of the season does it now? 'Tis, after all, what Halloween's all about.'

'But that's not all though is it? You told me that it was Samhain and the Witches' New Year and *that* is what we had planned for tonight, if I remember rightly. You were going to show me a ritual and I was really looking forward to it,' whined

6

Isis.

Minerva stared hard at Isis for a moment. 'By the good Lady, is that so? Well, my poor menopausal-struck memory does not serve me as well as it used to, then. But surely you weren't thinking of attending a ritual done up *like that* were you?'

'I thought I'd also enter into the spirit of Halloween,' said a crestfallen Isis. 'You wouldn't believe how difficult it was for me to venture round here dressed like this. I thought it was more than appropriate, but obviously, I was wrong.'

'Let's not get too hot and bothered about it all.' Minerva continued to fan herself furiously. 'We might as well drink to what's left of a good evening, though I think we'll refrain from rituals of any serious nature for the time being and just eat chocolate, drink brandy and be merry. What do you say?' Minerva raised her glass aloft and passed another to Isis.

'I have to say it sounds like a plan, but I would seriously like to learn more about these Pagan ways. After wasting so much of my time with Derek, it's high time I turned over a new leaf for good, don't you think?'

'I'll drink to that, Isis. Thank the Goddess for that Molly Maid woman, even if her un-maidenly behaviour did bring your marriage to an end. Without it, our paths may never have crossed and we would never have become belly-dancing buddies, would we?'

'Yes, you're right, Minerva, it's a lot of fun and now that I've changed my name, too, I feel so different, you wouldn't believe it!' She knocked back the rest of her drink and banged the glass so hard on the table that Minerva jumped back with a start.

'I think it's the best thing you've ever done, Isis, since I've known you, that is. I told you that changing your name would help things along, magically-speaking, of course. Now look at you!' She narrowed her eyes at her friend. 'And, seeing as you're dressed to kill, shall I be so bold as to invite any other tricky treaters into the lab for some *'crafty operations'*? What do you think?' She leaned across the table and pulled the green, warty nose back into position with a sharp tug.

'Minerva, you're the Devil incarnate at times...'

'Just a bit of fun, Ice, and by the way, he's one of my favourite cards.' She was soon unravelling a bundle of red velvet to reveal her treasured tarot cards. Finding the Devil, she propped him up against the brandy bottle and smiled. 'Not such a bad chap, you know, merely untamed, that's all. The bottom line is – few escape his clutches. None of us are without our dark side, are we?'

'I suppose not,' said Isis. 'So he's not all bad, then?' 'Absolutely *not,*' snapped Minerva. 'Just greatly misunderstood, that's all.'

'I know exactly how he feels then.'

'Oh yes! It's hot all right, in those burning hell fires,' said Minerva, fanning herself with the Devil and reaching for the brandy. 'You build up a terrible thirst in a place like that.'

'I don't doubt that for a minute,' said Isis, looking more lopsided than ever.

'Good,' said the green-shiny-faced Minerva. 'Ronnie'll be back from the stables soon. Let's get on with the celebrations.'

* * *

Ronnie felt sick. So sick, that she might have to get off her horse and just vomit right there alongside the bridle path. With slow deliberation, she looked around and wondered just how she was going to get down. Bob Marley was no small animal, but a big Welsh cob, with a backside like a tabletop and shaggy, black

8

dreadlocks for a mane. She hated the dry, matted things, but she loved Bob with a passion. She told him everything.

Big, black, tufty ears flicked back and forth as she poured out every corner of her heart and he never minded, never judged or criticized. He was the perfect listener.

Oh God, it's coming, she thought, as Bob spooked at a bogeyman in the hawthorn hedge. Without further ado, Ronnie swung her right leg up and over the huge, shaggy crest in front of her and slid down to the ground. As soon as she hit the soft mud beneath her, up it came. With one hand hanging on to the rein and the other hanging on to her own ponytail, she retched until she could retch no more.

Fumbling for a tissue, she screwed up her eyes in disgust. Yuk! And not even a night out to justify such a state. It was a good job no-one was about to witness such a pathetic sight.

Bob pawed at the ground, reminding her that he'd seen it all. In between deposits, she turned her head towards him. 'Oh Bob, what's a poor girl to do?'

This time he stamped and splattered mud at her with his dinner-plate feet. Ronnie felt the wet earth hit her cheek and smiled. 'Okay, I get it.'

She looked about for a fallen log, something to use as a spring- board for remounting. The track was narrow, with over-hanging bushes and nothing but the uneven trenches of muddy bog.

With great effort and a deep breath, she gathered up the reins and found the dangling stirrup with her left boot, now coated thick with mud. It kept slipping as the horse began to fidget and side step away from her.

'Bob...*stand!*'

Unused to such loud and pleading tones from his mistress;

Bob did what most horses do when they're unsure of what the hell's going on. He took off.

Fortunately for Ronnie, her slippery boot slid out and saved her, but she failed to keep the reins as the nervous animal pulled away and they burned through her fingers in spite of the gloves.

'Shit!'

She grabbed a nearby soggy bush for balance and watched her horse charge off down the track; stirrups, reins and dreadlocks flying as he headed for the road.

Ronnie's weakened body came alive with a sudden burst of adrenalin. It surged through her as she forgot herself and ran...through the squelching mud and down the track. She had to reach Bob.

Horses are strange creatures of flight and fancy, and farting. Usually they do these things separately, but the runaway was taking great delight in doing all three at once. His long, unkempt tail spouted upright like a fountain and expelled air loudly from underneath. His behaviour – odd though it may have appeared to anyone who was un-horsey – was actually quite normal for a cob with the wind up his tail.

However, on this particular day of vomiting and mud (both of which he'd had enough of), fortunately, something slowed down Bob and his rather sharp exit. Exactly *what* was not clear to the animal at first, as he hurtled along at breakneck speed. His main priority was running *from* the enemy without any idea of what he was running *to.*

Such are the instinctive traits of the equine species.

Now, to the human eye, a person with two dogs is...a person with two dogs. But, to a highly strung horse on the run, a person with two dogs is worse than a bogeyman in the hedge. It is, in fact, a monster on the move with two little monsters who are going to kill you.

Thankfully, Bob was blessed with a certain amount of self-preservation. As the moving monsters drew closer, he slammed on the brakes just a few feet away. The big monster started to shout and wave its arms around while the smaller ones darted around, making horrid, yapping noises.

He snorted loudly as all the monsters drew together and stopped moving. After a brief moment of silence, the yapping started again. Bob wasn't taking any nonsense and followed it up with an abrupt about-turn (a demi-pirouette Ronnie would have been proud of) and another mad dash away. It was all too much…death threats can affect horses like this.

Ronnie slowed up as she caught sight of Bob heading back down the track towards her. She thanked the heavens for whatever had caused his hasty retreat and immediately stuck her arms out at right angles. Fleeting thoughts of human sacrifice were overcome with relief as she found she could almost touch the wet bushes on either side, leaving no room for further escape.

Keeping her voice low, she spoke to the nervous animal as he pranced at a fast trot through the mud. 'Whoa there, fella, whoa there… It's okay, slowly now, whoa there, boy…'

His owner's familiar tones brought comfort to Bob's jangled nerves as he slowed down with each step.

He was safe now.

Ronnie approached her horse with a gentleness that disguised the adrenalin still coursing through her veins. He responded by lowering his head and billowing hot air into her outstretched palm with his velvety nostrils. She was quick to reach out with the other hand and quietly took the dangling rein off the ground.

She'd got him.

Pressing her head against the matted dreadlocks, she breathed a long sigh of relief into this strange, sensitive creature, who constantly reminded her how precious life was, just by being precious himself. Funny how the threat of losing something jolts you awake and how an animal can teach that without even trying.

What *wasn't* funny, however, was the figure walking towards them with dogs (now on leads) hugged closely to his side. She'd know that swagger anywhere, the scruffy charm and the grin.

Joe.

She stiffened.

'Hey, Ron, you all right?' He looked pale.

Ronnie curled her fingers hard around the reins. 'We're okay, thanks…just. Bob got a fright, that's all.'

'You fell off?'

'No, that's not what happened. I dropped something and got off to pick it up and he got spooked and ran off.'

'He was heading pretty quick for the road!' Joe bent down to pat the two spaniels on red alert by his side. 'But he soon pulled himself up when he saw us.'

'Well what do you expect? You're the *monsters*.' Ronnie's eyes widened.

It was good to hear Joe laugh.

'As long as you're all right, that's the main thing.' He sounded relieved. 'Can't have my best mate pegging out on me now, can I?' His eyes creased up and twinkled at her before dropping to the ground. An awkward silence fell over them, interrupted by the low hoot of an owl in the trees.

'How *are* you, Joe? Haven't seen you in ages. Mum and I have been wondering.'

'Yeah, all right, thanks,' he said quickly. 'Back at work now.
It's not too bad. Busy with the boats, as usual.' 'How long
have you been at the marina now?'

'Must be getting on for three years, I suppose… Keeps me
out of trouble and I like it, which helps.' He looked across at
her. 'Getting back on my feet slowly, Ron.'

'Glad to hear it. Are you doing any playing?' She'd seen the
poster in the village.

'The band's got a gig this Saturday, down at the Old Druid…'
he faltered. 'First one for a while…since Mum died, anyway.'

Joe looked so vulnerable, it hurt Ronnie, and yet she was
pleased he'd mentioned Eve. He had the exact look of her, with
his cheeky grin under the mop of thick, mousey hair. Oh and
the eyes…it was quite uncanny. She hadn't ever known anyone
with cancer before, nor did she ever want to again.

Poor Eve. The whole thing had frightened her, and although
they'd said a year was not that long, as far as she was concerned
any length of time with that wicked illness was far too long for
anyone. She couldn't imagine Joe without his music – it was
his saving grace – she was glad he was still into it.

'Oh, that's great, Joe, I'll definitely come along to that…and
I'm sure Mum would like to come too, if she can tear herself
away from her cards, candles and crystals, of course. It'll do
her good to have a break.'

'Is she still doing her tarot readings over the phone?'

'Oh yeah…and anywhere else she can do readings. *'It puts
pennies in the cauldron Rhiannon.'* You know how she is.'

Joe was laughing. 'I do indeed. Power to Minerva, oh wild
and witchy woman! Still as mad as ever, eh, Ron?'

'Never a dull moment in our household…especially at the
moment. Mum's favourite time of year, of course. Samhain,

or Halloween to the uninitiated. It's good to get out, though.' She looked at Bob.

'Know what you mean, Ron, the great outdoors.' He opened his arms wide and looked up, then down again at the dogs. 'Better be getting on; these two need to let off a bit more steam.' The spaniels bounced up and down, a black-and-white blur of floppy ears and tails and frantic, darting eyes. 'Really good to see you and Mr Marley… Wanna leg up?' he nodded towards Bob.

'Thanks.' Ronnie gathered up the reins and Bob began to mark time with his front legs. 'Stand, lad.'

Joe released the dogs, instructing them to wait with a hand signal and walked quietly up to the horse and rider. He went up to Bob's head and, holding the reins, held out his right arm to catch Ronnie's leg.

It wasn't the most graceful of mounts. Ronnie was not the feather-light fairy she dreamed of being. Her stocky frame covered big bones.

'*Built for comfort, not speed,*' Grandad would say with great affection. But the words had stuck with Ronnie and, although she was far from overweight, her size did upset her. She battled with it constantly, regardless of her mother's reassurance: 'You have *nothing* to worry about, darling. Just like your namesake, the Goddess Rhiannon – beautiful and *strong*. You're just right.'

Well, she didn't feel too strong at the moment, especially after releasing all the contents of her stomach. Not a bad thing really, she thought.

'Blimey, Ron, make an effort will you?' She was a dead weight against him.

'Sorry,' she mumbled into Bob's dreadlocks. 'Never did have much spring!'

Laughing nervously and after much pushing and pulling, Ronnie scrambled into the saddle.

'Thanks,' she said.

They looked at each other and burst out laughing, startling all three animals.

'Like I was saying, it's good to see you, Ron. Catch up again on Saturday!' Joe raised a hand as he walked off. The dogs ran along in front, tails waving rapidly like flags and noses to the ground.

Ronnie felt better.

She drew a long breath in and the cold air hit her...a blast of late autumn, carrying the promise of winter while the earth prepared for her great slumber. Naked branches reached out where rusty leaves had fallen and surrendered themselves to the ground. Bonfire smoke seeped through the trees and clung to hair and clothes and animal fur.

She looked at her watch as she gathered up the reins and nudged Bob forwards – time to head back to the yard. The nights were drawing in quickly and it would be getting dark soon. Her mother sprang into her mind, along with pumpkins and cobwebs and ghostly goings-on.

'The ghoulies'll be out to get us if we're not careful, Bob,' she said.

The big, shaggy head nodded in agreement.

She really ought to sort out those dreadlocks.

2

Posh Bird and the Druid Fluid

The stable lights were already on when they got back. Steamy clouds rose from the muck heap and greeted them with an earthy stench. It was pure horse heaven to Ronnie.

The yard bustled with life as people milled about on the end of wheelbarrows, feed buckets toppling, head collars and haynets dangling from handles and shoulders. The nausea still gnawed at her stomach as she dismounted and led Bob to his stable, glad of its discreet position around the back.
Socializing was not what she had in mind.

Bob had just one other neighbour. The lovely Kismet was a lady of impeccable manners and a thoroughbred of the finest breeding. Quite how two such different animals found themselves next door to each other was beyond Ronnie, but it amused her. The small, delicate head of the grey, with her fine wisp of mane, made quite a contrast to the Roman-nosed cob and his coarse, black dreadlocks. They were the perfect lady and the tramp, the most unlikely of couples, although Kismet's owner, Sophia – being too much of a lady herself –

never mentioned it, and Ronnie appreciated her good manners.

As Ronnie made her way to the tack room, a wheelbarrow appeared around the corner, followed by Sophia. This was a lady with a horse and car to match. Her slick, dark-green Mini Cooper shone polish-perfect at all times, tempting Ronnie to cadge a lift whenever she could and indulge herself in its lush interior. She saw the sparkling dashboard, quadraphonic sound system and luxury oozing from every pore of its leather upholstery as having everything that her mother's Morris Minor did not. The style and quirks of Mr. Morris had worn thin with Ronnie over the years and his quaint appeal no longer had the same effect on her. There was only so much travelling in a car without heating or a sound system – and with a driver's door that refused to open – that anyone could put up with. Cold, impractical and downright embarrassing, Mr Morris had reduced Ronnie's tolerance levels to well below zero.

It was easy to see why she now preferred her friend's thoroughly modern Mini. And clearly, Sophia could well afford it, or at least Daddy-the-barrister could.

Sophia beamed at Ronnie. 'Hello, you! Nice ride?'

'Hi, Sophia. Yes, it was thanks. Cold out there, though. You're here early tonight, aren't you? You don't normally get here until at least six.'

'I know; that's because I never normally get time off uni, but I only had two lectures this morning. Done and dusted by lunchtime and back home by two.'

Thanks to your Mini hot rod, thought Ronnie.

'Just managed a lovely schooling session with Kizzy,' said Sophia. 'A complete darling, as usual.'

'Wish I could say the same for Mr. Marley, there.' Ronnie nodded at Bob, who - oblivious as most horses are to the mention of his name – was busy chomping away at his haynet.

'Hey Bob, what have you been up to?' Sophia called towards the munching sounds coming from the stable.

'Bob decided to get away from me and leg it up Blind Man's Path bridleway for the road. Luckily, a friend of mine stopped him or it could have been nasty,' said Ronnie.

'Did you come off him, then?' asked Sophia.

Ronnie hesitated. She didn't want to lie, as Sophia was hard wired to the truth – a side-effect of studying law – and besides, she didn't have the energy to make something up.

'No, actually... I...got off to be sick. Wasn't feeling too well; must've been something I ate.'

'I find that hard to believe, Ron; you have the constitution of an ox!'

The truth was she was right. And the truth, it appeared, was exactly what Sophia was going to get out of her.

'Remember all that food and drink you devoured at the stables' party the other week? You packed it away like a woman possessed. And, as *I remember*, you were completely fine the next day.'

Ronnie stared into the space behind Sophia, who was right, as usual.

Yes, the party...probably a good place to start. They always threw good parties at the stables, someone's birthday or leaving do.

But she hadn't felt like celebrating much...

It had all started earlier that day, as she was getting off the bus from college: she'd heard the laughter first, and then she'd seen them - Joe and some girl – some *posh bird* and, more than likely, the daughter of a boat owner. The feeling had crept under her skin, declaring itself in no uncertain terms... *You are jealous.*

She didn't understand it. She and Joe had been friends for years, just like brother and sister. She'd even looked up platonic in the dictionary. 'Love and friendship but *not* sexual,' had stared back at her, in black and white. So maybe things had changed. Maybe *she'd* changed?

'Magic is all about change.' Her mother's words called out from the ether.

But magical was *not* how she'd felt. Change was definitely afoot. Maybe one *posh bird* – daughter of a boat owner – was enough to make the difference. By the time she'd walked home, she had been confused and scared. And the party had been the perfect remedy of course.

Gavin had been there...apprentice farrier and stable hunk.

Gavin, of fair face and fine body... Oh God no, that was it!

'Ronnie,' Sophia touched her shoulder. 'You okay?'

The girls plopped on to the straw bale outside the stables and looked at the ground in front of them, avoiding each other's gaze.

Ronnie dug her fists deep into the stiff straw.

'Is there anything you'd like to talk about?' Sophia's voice was low. 'You're not...pregnant, are you?'

Ronnie didn't speak. Eventually, she turned to face her friend. 'How do you know I am?' she whispered.

'Because I'm not bloody stupid and *you are!*'

'Don't, Sophia,' she pleaded. 'Surely it can't happen on a one-night stand... Can it?'

'Are you daft as well as mad, Ron? Of course it can... Did you not *think?*'

'I'd had quite a bit to drink, so you could say I was drinking instead of...'

19

'Thinking?'

'Don't make this worse than it already is,' Ronnie groaned. 'I can't believe I was so stupid myself…but I was upset and I just wanted to numb it all out.'

'Numb what out?'

'The pain… Okay, jealousy, I suppose. I saw my friend Joe with a…girl. We've known each other years and…'

'Who, the girl?'

'No, not the girl - Joe! We're like brother and sister.'

'Purely platonic, then.'

Patronizing bitch, thought Ronnie.

'Yes, that's all…until now. Don't ask me why it's changed.' She shrugged. 'It just has…'

'Look, Ronnie, it's not worth beating yourself up about, really it's not.' Sophia felt rotten. It was a friend Ronnie needed, not a lawyer. 'What's important now is what you are going to do about it.'

She stopped suddenly and looked at the girl next to her. The girl she had known only since she'd arrived at the yard a few months ago. The girl who'd made her feel welcome, shown her round and given her the run-down on everyone and everything. The girl who made her laugh, with her sunny smile, quick wit and big heart.

The girl who'd gone and got herself up the duff.

'Can you remember what happened at the party?' asked Sophia. 'I have to say, I was glad to get out when I did; it was all getting a bit raucous for me, plus I had that dressage competition the next day, if you remember.'

'Yes,' Ronnie sighed. 'I can remember you going…just.'

'You were particularly drunk by then, swaying at the side of the muck heap as I was looking for my car keys on the ground somewhere. And then you found them.'

'Did I?'

'Yes! They were in your jeans pocket. You took them off me when I said I was driving back later and you would *not* accept that I wasn't drinking. Kept trying to make me drink that really strong cider, remember? By that time, of course, you'd had a good few yourself!'

Ronnie stifled a giggle as the fog began to clear in her mind. 'I remember that, yes…didn't touch the sides. That's the trouble with that stuff…good old Druid Fluid…goes down far too easy.'

'You can't blame the drink, Ron!'

'Oh yes, I can. Evil stuff, drink…should be a warning on the bottles,' complained Ronnie, shooting Sophia a rebellious look.

'There *is* a warning, you idiot. It's written in the alcohol percentage on the side.' She nudged her elbow into Ronnie's side. 'Honestly, once you've gone past the halfway mark, there's no stopping you and woe betide anyone who tries to do so. I gave up that night and *that's* why I buggered off early, too, not just the fact I had an early start but because *you*, Rhiannon, were clearly on a roll and I'd had enough,' Sophia was getting all superior again. 'You can be downright obnoxious when you've had a few too many!'

'So you went and left me. Thanks, matey.' Ronnie hissed.

'Don't be absurd! Shifting the blame will not get you anywhere,' scoffed Sophia. 'You'll be telling me next you were raped, for God's sake: either that or the victim of an immaculate conception, one of the two.'

'I'd rather the latter of the two, thanks: I prefer angels to devils,' snapped Ronnie.

'I'm sorry, Ron, but sometimes you take it too far.'

'Oh and you don't? No, of course you don't, Sophia. You're

far too clever.' Ronnie caught Sophia's hurt expression. 'Oh look, *I'm sorry*, I'm bloody sorry, all right? What's going on? Why are we arguing? I don't want this!'

'Neither do I,' agreed Sophia. 'Although it's perfectly normal, I think…under the circumstances. When emotions are high, it happens all the time.'

'I guess it just did,' sighed Ronnie. 'Absolutely.' Sophia smiled. 'It did indeed.'

The two girls sat in silence.

The sort of silence that friends can be in together, without feeling they need to break it somehow with superfluous drivel or daft banter.

They were better than that.

They were teetering on the edge of real friendship, although they didn't realise it yet, but they would in time. Finding themselves in unknown territory, they had arrived in no-man's land, where a night of drunken abandonment stretched around it like barbed wire, choking it with fear. They were scared, but found some consolation in each other's company. Friends become closer when they share hard times.

And horses can be counted on to interrupt in the rudest of ways. The girls were startled out of their heavy silence by a loud raspberry, rippling out from Bob's stable.

Trust Bob. Divine timing was definitely one of his fortes. It was hard to tell who was more surprised, the girls or the horse, who looked up with sudden alarm, dreadlocks flapping.

'Nice one, Mr. Marley,' called out Sophia. 'We much appreciate the welcome break!'

The straw bale toppled forwards underneath them as they keeled over in a fit of giggles.

It was a well-timed and much needed tonic.

* * *

The sweet smell of molasses filled the early evening air as Ronnie mixed up the feeds for the horses. The colourful mix of grains, combined with the slushy beet pulp and molasses, was more than enough to tempt even the poorest of equine appetites. The sticky food stuck to the broken end of the broom handle as she stirred it round in trance-like fashion. This small, mundane act was her therapy as she lost herself in the moment, right there. She did the same thing morning and evening, every day of the week, from one month to the next, as well as the mucking out and the riding and the many other jobs that are involved with looking after horses.

It was a labour of love that she never tired of.

Five years had gone in a flash since her fourteenth birthday, when the gift from her father in the form of Bob had trotted gaily into her life. Mum said it was to lessen her pain and his guilt after leaving them, what else? A horse was the perfect consolation prize to win her over, while her father shacked up with some floozy halfway across the country.

Ronnie had given up analyzing it; her mother did enough of that and, in the end, she wasn't sure it did any good. People split up, relationships didn't always work out and yes, it was hard sometimes, but probably more so for her mother than it was for Ronnie. Poor Mum had suffered, taken it badly and never looked at another man since Dad went. That was the trouble.

She, at least, had Bob. The gap left by an unhappy man had been filled with a happy horse. She knew who she'd rather have, and – with no disrespect to her father, as she loved him dearly – he was better off where he was. She still got to see him once every couple of months or so, when he came down with Laura, his girlfriend – and it was just fine. They stayed at the Old Druid pub in the village, she joined them for meals and they came down to see Bob, and it all worked out. Mum was the one with the problem, and five years had not lessened the blow. A new man in her life could well be the answer... Ronnie mused over this with a smile.

She slid the horses' feeds into the stables and bolted them up for the night, locked up the little tack room next door and, with a quick glance behind her, made her way down through the main yard and out into the car park at the front. Sophia should be back by now.

Right on cue, the dazzling headlights bumped their way into the makeshift car park of undulating water holes and mud. Ronnie stopped and waited, sliding her boot beneath the murky water of a puddle to see how deep it was and gently patting the sole of her foot up and down. The little green hot rod emerged from the darkness, with Sophia staring blankly ahead, casually raising her fingers above the top of the steering wheel as she pulled up beside her.

'Did you get it?' Ronnie said to the dashboard as she climbed in and carefully placed her muddy boots on the neatly folded plastic bag on the floor.

Sophia didn't say a word, but reached into the glove compartment and pulled out a small paper bag, which she handed to her friend. Ronnie took a sharp breath in as she pulled out the slim packet inside and stared at the pregnancy test kit.

'When do I do it?'

'In the morning, first thing.' 'What if...?'

'No 'what ifs'. Just do it, Ron, the sooner the better.'

'How long do I have to wait?'

'You don't; it's instant, pretty much. There'll be a line that appears…if you *are*, that is.' Her frostiness unnerved Ronnie. 'Do you fancy a drink? I could do with one myself,' said Sophia, checking her mirror.

'Good thinking, Batman.' Ronnie managed a weak smile as she clicked her seatbelt into place. 'Don't mind if I do.'

* * *

Leaving Sophia's car at her house, the two girls walked to the pub – a very convenient stone's throw away. The fire crackled and spat from the hearth in the dingy interior of the Old Druid. The less-than-crowded room with its dark, intimate corners gave them all the privacy they needed. It never seemed to change and Ronnie loved the feel of the place. It transported her to another time, way back, before the modern world took its hold over the country folk and pushed them headlong into the towns and cities. Way before it sucked them into the fast lane of life and its constant traffic and noise. Before it took them away from the fields and the forests and the birdsong… Before it seduced them with faster and bigger and better.

She loved the tiny alcoves and low beams of solid oak, worn smooth with the years. She loved the sparse furnishings and the picture of the old Druid priest over the fireplace, arms outstretched to the moon and surveying the room from his circle of standing stones.

She also loved the cider.

'Cheers, good friend,' said Ronnie, as she raised her glass first to Sophia and then to the old Druid above the fire. 'And to you, Sir, your very good health.' She was almost sure the sparkle in his eyes twinkled back at her.

25

'They might not have much else in here, but this stuff makes up for it.' Sophia smiled at the golden liquid in her glass.

'Can't beat the old Druid Fluid,' said Ronnie. 'They brew it here, you know.'

'Anyway, Ron…' Sophia frowned. 'Are you sure about…you know…Gavin. Are you *sure* it actually happened?'

'Well, as sure as we're sitting here and Old Man Druid's up there.' Ronnie stared at the picture. 'It was a moment of madness, fuelled by a mixture of self-pity and a kind of weird revenge that came over me.'

'Not to mention *that* stuff.' Sophia raised her eyebrows at Ronnie's glass.

'Well, yes, not the best influence, as we've concluded so far.'

'Where…did it happen?'

'In the hay barn.' Ronnie's tone was strangely calm. 'Right at the back and, if you must know, I was a willing participant and I didn't care. I knew Gavin liked me; he'd been giving me the eye for ages. So that's it.' She downed her cider and made her way to the bar. 'Another?'

'Oh, go on, then,' said Sophia. 'Sod it.'

'Another two, please, Ernie!' Ronnie strained over the bar and called down to the other end, where the landlord finally appeared. She couldn't help noticing he had rather a peculiar likeness to the Old Druid himself. In fact, thought Ronnie, it probably really *is* the old boy reincarnated. Who was to say it wasn't? She chuckled inwardly as Ernie took his time over the refills and her eyes wandered around the bar area.

The poster caught her eye straight away and her heart lurched. Only one person could do that to her. Joe's face stared back at her…there he was, with his band of merry music men – the Planet Reapers. She'd chosen the name, after he'd asked her advice one evening at rehearsals.

'What do you reckon on a name then, Ron? We need one; we got our first gig coming up.'

'Well, considering the state you were in tonight – herbal recreational time seems to combine well with rehearsals – I'd say you were off the planet so…how about the Planet Reapers?'

'Nice one, Ron, that'll do.' Joe had grinned at her.

That was it. One satisfied customer. No deliberating for hours. No seeking approval from any quarter. No checking to see if anyone else had the same name. It didn't matter. A decision made then and there. They all loved the name, too.

Joe and the Planet Reapers were born.

She thought what a great photo it was. The lads caught in full, musical flow and clearly rocking it out as only they knew how. A wild-eyed Stag with hair and drumsticks flying at the back while, bent over his bass, was a shaven-headed Rocco and, striking a Hendrix pose in the front with his precious Telecaster, was Joe.

There it was, in black and white…they were playing at the Old Druid that Saturday. It was bound to be a good night and she wanted to be there. She'd been there right from the start, cheering them on at the sidelines, from playing to one man and his dog, to performing in places that had been heaving from all sides.

She turned to Sophia. 'You'll come on Saturday, won't you? Joe's band is playing here. Should be a good night!'

Sophia caught the excitement in her voice. 'You mean…Joe… The one you…? Oh…yes, I'd love to. Could do with a night out. What sort of music is it?'

'A mixture really: a lot of rock covers, but they do their own stuff too and it's great. Joe's a good songwriter…' Her voice trailed off.

This was madness, thought Sophia. Shoving things under the carpet was not her style, but she would go along with it. She'd become fond of Ronnie in a very short time and appreciated her friendship. She was clearly a bit of a wild child and surely it wouldn't hurt to let her own hair down and join her. Besides, she didn't know that many people in the village, whereas Ronnie did, and she quite liked the idea of getting out a bit more. Saturday nights could be lonely in a village where one was new on the scene.

They drank further into the night and munched on crisps and peanuts and laughed and joked and wobbled to the toilet and back and finally got up to leave. As they did, a couple came in and approached the bar, passing the girls on the way.

Her eyesight and reflexes were not at their best and Ronnie managed to knock her glass over, spilling the last of its contents on to the female of the couple. This did not bode well for Ronnie.

'Oh!' The female cried. 'Thanks very much!'

Ronnie was too busy to hear or notice, caught up in an attempt to remove her jacket from the back of a chair. This was no easy feat, considering the chair appeared to have claimed the jacket in a stranglehold and wasn't letting go.

'Ron, what *are* you up to?' She recognized that voice.

'I'm soaked!' said the female, turning to the voice for support. Ronnie looked in the direction of the voice. Joe again. How come she hadn't seen him for ages and then he appeared three times (she was including the poster) in one day?

And the female? Well it had to be *Posh Bird* – daughter of boat owner – of course.

Great.

Posh Bird was puce in the face and Joe wore a smirk of what appeared to be a mixture of concern and amusement. An odd combination, she thought, but nevertheless appealing in a charming sort of way. At least he was gentlemanly enough to demonstrate the former and friendly enough to feel the latter.

How considerate of him.

'Oh shit… I'm sorry,' she said to Posh Bird. 'Didn't mean to…'

'No, of course you didn't, I'm sure,' said Posh Bird through clenched teeth.

What a horror, thought Sophia, heading off in search of a cloth.

Ronnie fumbled around in her jacket pocket and brought out a grubby handkerchief, which she passed to Posh Bird in her most humble, apologetic manner. Looking at Joe and with lips tightly pursed, Posh Bird took it and dabbed at her wet clothes, before handing the soiled specimen back to Ronnie.

It was an awkward moment, to say the least.

'Well, Joe, fancy seeing you…*again.*' Ronnie couldn't help herself.

'Penny,' Joe's eyes were fixed on Posh Bird, 'this is *Ronnie*, an old friend of mine… We grew up together,' he added quickly. As drunk as she was, this was not lost on Ronnie.

You bastard she told him silently.

'Oh, *Penny*! Is that short for Pen-el-o-pee?' Ronnie thrust out a sweaty hand. 'Charmed, I'm sure!'

Ignoring the gesture, Posh Bird shot a filthy look at all of them. 'Right. Well, pleased to meet you,' she said, quickly regaining her composure. 'See you around some time.'

And she strutted off to the bar.

'Yeah, whatever,' said Ronnie, her hands boldly forming a

W-shape in mid air behind her.

'Ron...no need for that,' Joe glared at her. 'You've had a bit too much. Maybe going home's not a bad idea.'

'Per...raps I should and per...raps I shouldn't,' said Ronnie, clasping her chin and beginning to sway.

Sophia finished her cloth duties and moved in swiftly, taking a firm grip of Ronnie's elbow and aiming for the door.

'I'm Sophia, by the way,' she called behind her. 'Nice to meet you!'

'Oh...yeah, and you,' said a dazed Joe.

'We're coming on Saturday...to see your band,' said Sophia, pushing a reluctant Ronnie outside. 'See you then. Bye!'

Posh Bird shot a dark glare at Joe from the bar.

'Mine's a large one,' he called across the room, looking up at the old Druid on the wall.

And, for a moment, he could've sworn he winked at him.

3

Lucifer, the Hanged Man and a Man of the Cloth

Minerva was having one of her men-o-whats-it moments. The thing was, she wasn't particularly aware that it *was* one of those moments. As far as she was concerned, it was as normal as the moment gets when one is firmly in the grip of a terrible migraine one is trying to cure by performing a headstand up against a greenhouse on a cold, wintry morning.

She grimaced in pain, certain that Thor himself was raining down blows on her poor head, and under the great hammer of such a merciless God, she felt powerless. The headstand was just one of a multitude of remedies she tried on frequent occasions along the menopausal highway to hell – a perilous, hormonal journey she traversed far too often at the expense of her own sanity (or what was left of it) and any other innocent bystanders. Minerva battled fiercely through the rocky terrain by natural means alone. After all, isn't that what Witches did?

Her devout commitment to her magical hat was honourable, although draining on many levels, especially when it came to her health. She was a bit of a martyr and in walking a path of natural being and doing, hated the thought of depending on anything that was *unnatural*.

As she saw it, anything that was man made and not of the earth, was just a crutch to lean on when there was so much more she could do for herself. Like making disgusting green smoothies, drinking the foulest tasting herbal tonics or forsaking every luxury in her diet (as long as it wasn't caffeine, chocolate or alcohol); *anything* in fact that might taste barely edible, apart from looking and smelling like the local sewer.

All this was, of course, if she felt like it. Very often, Minerva didn't. But she would face these trying times and whatever men-o-what-sit episode she was going through with a brave face, usually at the expense of some poor, unsuspecting witness. However, it seemed to work that one man's torture was another's entertainment, and each episode seemed to produce variations on the same theme. She blamed the hormones, of course.

It was as simple as that.

This meant that, whatever murderous tendency came over her, whatever volcanic eruption of turbulent emotions spewed over the nearest innocent party, they would find themselves rudely awakened and discover they weren't innocent at all. In fact, it was all a figment of their imagination. And *this* is what any woman unfortunate enough to be suffering from the ghastly menopausal disease will tell you, in no uncertain terms: it is NOT their fault.

It's everybody else's.

Another reason for the headstand by the greenhouse that morning was the Hanged Man of course. He seemed to be one of her favourite tarot characters at this particular time and, after all, they shared a certain amount of altered perception, which was probably why. Besides, hanging out with this chap seemed like a good thing to do. They appeared to have a lot in common and upside-down-ness was definitely one of them. She just couldn't think straight when a migraine hit her and beneath the surface of a pounding head, her psychic juices bubbled and simmered.

So she had picked a card...

Tell me what to do! Had been her instruction to the universe as she proceeded with the first shuffle of the day. And, quite clearly the universe did.

Short of hanging herself upside down from the nearest tree, which she decided was not a good idea (too many nosey neighbours spoil a good spell); Minerva was stuck for options at first. But, after the first fully-loaded coffee meditation of the day, and seeking only the attention of the universe, it came to her in a flash and a crash. The former came from the divine as she understood it and the latter was something of a more earthly nature - Lucifer committing murder in the greenhouse.

Lucifer was a huge, black, tom cat, sporting one-and-a-half ears and various bald spots about his person: evidence of his many fights around the local village. He had turned up in the garden, one wet, Saturday night, to find Minerva communing with the dark side of the moon in the rain. The bedraggled waif appeared as if from the sky itself and fell at her feet in a most peculiar, un-cat-like sprawl.

'Oh, my Goddess, you are fallen from the heavens...you poor angel!' Minerva's dramatic tones had rung round the dark garden as she raised her arms to the cosmos. 'No less than a shining star in our midst!'

'No,' his bruised and battered body cried out to her, *'I am just*

a black cat without a home...and you are a home without a black cat.'

Fortunately, it was perfectly clear to Minerva - and after the shock of the creature's arrival had eventually subsided – love blossomed at second or possibly third sight. Whatever it was, the ugly thing had a certain, pitiful charm that couldn't be ignored and she'd been hooked from that moment on. There was no denying it, Lucifer was a magical beast.

However, this did not excuse him from being the vicious and unfriendly brute the passing of time revealed him to be. Neither did it make him popular (although it did wonders for his street credibility among the other cats in the village) but he did turn out to be a great ratter. And, as the garden backed on to a farmer's field of ditches and dirt, with rats as frequent and unwelcome visitors, he proved a useful addition and earned his place in the Crafty family.

Yes, Lucifer's landing was truly a gift from the heavens.

When the flash happened (moments of sudden inspiration would often accompany a freshly-picked card), Minerva slammed her coffee down, splashing the Hanged Man in the face, and ran outside in the direction of the crash. There, prostrate on the greenhouse floor, was Lucifer, with a large rat pinned between paw and ground. This was no menial game of cat and mouse. Shards of bloodied glass lay in a jagged heap around them and the victor claimed his prize with a final lunge at his victim...finishing it.

Minerva let out a high-pitched cry at the ugly scene. Perhaps it was Lucifer who had infected her with those murderous tendencies? Perhaps it wasn't her hormones at all? Or perhaps she was just confused.

She wasn't sure whether to feel cross, repulsed or relieved at the sight before her and, as she was used to dealing with mixed emotions on a regular basis, it came quite naturally to combine them all.

'Luce, you great *brute* of a cat,' she cried, 'you could at least have some respect! My greenhouse is *not* a boxing ring... Oh, my Goddess, what a horrid piece of vermin, but you *are* a clever boy... Yes, you are.'

Lucifer took it all in his stride and, ignoring the screaming Minerva, picked up his prize with great care and slunk off to the back field with the grey fangs of dead rodent dangling from his mouth. She didn't want to think or know about what he planned to do with it, but it gave her an idea...

She knew it was a sign.

Luck was not something she believed in, but patterns and signs, she thought, showed up in all things, if you just looked closely enough. Events strung themselves together from threads of the past to the future in the most magical of ways. Woven by the Goddess of synchronicity herself, the web of life was an amazing tapestry of symbolic language – if one cared enough to study and understand it – give or take the odd tangle here and there.

Of course...that's it! She thought, as the monster-migraine, the Hanged Man and the greenhouse spun and merged as one inside her head.

It was obvious.

* * *

Ronnie woke in a hazy blur and convinced herself she was dreaming – although, if the screams were anything to go by, it was more like a nightmare. Cocooned in her duvet, she buried her head as the cries continued, until she realised where and who it was coming from.

The garden and her mother.

As much as she wanted to leap out of bed, she couldn't: hangovers could leave a girl wasted and vertically challenged at the best of times. Eventually, the screaming died down to a low murmur and she managed to drag herself to the window and peer out at the garden below. Quite what her mother was doing, she wasn't sure, but it looked like some kind of headstand against the greenhouse and, by the looks of it, she was perilously close to falling through the open window at the top. Enjoying the coldness of the window pane against her forehead, Ronnie looked closer and realised one of Minerva's feet was actually stuck *in* the window.

Shouting was out of the question. Her head would definitely explode if she did that. She pulled on her dressing gown and made a slow and deliberate descent to the garden and her mother. The cold air rushed to meet her as she crunched her way through the grass and over to the greenhouse.

'Mum...*what* exactly are you doing?'

'Ronnie, thank God. Can you please remove that horrid, great monster in front of me NOW!'

'What monster?'

'The one right under my nose,' Minerva said, through gritted teeth. 'Get the spade and DO SOMETHING!'

In all fairness, the spider was no small beast and, knowing her mother's phobia only too well, Ronnie acted quickly. She slid the spade towards the spider *and* her mother, regretting the foolish move straight away. Consequently, the hysterical screams from Minerva, pinned in catatonic state to the wobbling greenhouse (now swaying in a dangerous manner), reached a deafening pitch.

'Where is it? *Where is it?*' The spider ran for cover to the herb patch, leaving Minerva gasping, 'Ronnie... GET IT!'

'Mum, it's okay. It's gone. *It's gone!*'

Ronnie grabbed her mother's ankles, carefully extracting one of them from the open window and guiding them down with the greatest of care. This was no easy feat as the rigor-mortified Minerva was not the most co-operative of subjects.

'Mum, it's all right, relax. Just relax your legs, *please!*'

Minerva, by this point could hold on no longer and slumped to the ground in a heap.

'Come on, let's get inside, Mum. I'll make us a coffee,' said Ronnie, helping her mother on to her feet.

'With that chamber of horrors behind us,' said a shivering Minerva. 'I think something a little stronger, don't you, dear?' Hugging her dressing gown tightly around her and swallowing hard, Ronnie couldn't think of anything worse.

* * *

Although a little shaky, Minerva was relieved to find the pounding and throbbing in her head had gone. The spell had worked. Dazed but nevertheless grateful for the spider's contribution, she felt certain the Goddess Arachne had spun her magic to release and transform the dark energy of fear that had plagued her for most of her life.

Arachnophobia was a terrible curse.

Perhaps she must do this to rid herself of *any* phobia – face the fear and do it anyway – only next time maybe not up against a greenhouse. Quite what that translated into, in terms of the spider thing, she didn't know. She had no intention of repeating that again in a hurry – but she knew one thing for sure… It had shocked the hammer-headed monster out of her head and into oblivion, where it belonged.

Yes, that was it, rattling those wretched hormones and their rude, unscrupulous behaviour with fear and hysteria was the answer – with the help of the spider Goddess, of course. Minerva felt a familiar quiver of apprehension and a sense of great power returning. She could smell it.

Magic was in the air.

'I think it's time for a little spell casting,' she said to Ronnie, from the cosy and horizontal world of the sofa. 'A little word in the universe's ear.'

'What for?' Ronnie winced as she moved her head and peeked at her mother over the top of her cup.

'I need some excitement…some sparkle! Life has become far too mundane, Ronnie, and I'm constantly battling with the hormone horrors and this beastly men-o-what-sit disease. It's a terrible curse. I need something else to focus on, before I go completely insane.'

Ronnie sighed. 'I presume this has something to do with what was going on in the garden, Mother?'

'Of course it has. I was trying to get rid of a migraine, *Rhiannon…*' Minerva stroked the side of her temple. 'The Hanged Man appeared just at the right time, as did the rat and Lucifer in the greenhouse.'

Ronnie thought it sounded more like a game of Cluedo than a divinely-timed event. However, she was used to her mother's ways – it was all perfectly normal. She'd grown up with what some people might view as odd and weird, but to her it was just Mother and the magic. They could think what they liked; she didn't care and wasn't about to analyse it now, not with her banging head.

She fixed her attention on Minerva, who was a pretty good distraction: wild hair, wide-eyes and well on the way to being pie-eyed, given the amount of brandy she was knocking back.

'What are you talking about, Mum?'

'There are no coincidences, only *minor or major acts of magic*. It's always in the cards. You're a bit slow on the uptake this morning, Ronnie.'

'Oh, go on, then…enlighten me.'

'All three came together, you see… It was the universe telling me.'

'To do what? To stand on your head on a freezing cold morning, in the garden, up against the greenhouse and scream?'

'*That* was not part of the plan, Rhiannon, as I'm sure you're aware. The spider appeared *after* I'd taken great pains to position myself. Scream was the only thing I could do. I was frozen in horror and in a complete state of shock, if you must know!'

'Yes, I could *see* that, but you're okay now, right?'

'Yes I am – and thanks to you, darling, for rescuing me – but the point is I'm more than okay. The migraine has gone completely…vanished into the ether!' Minerva waved her arms. 'I feel absolutely fine.'

Thanks to the brandy, thought Ronnie.

'Well, I'm glad, Mum, that's great.' Ronnie was flagging and not in quite the same magical mood Minerva was. 'So, what exactly are you saying?'

'What I'm saying is that the combination of all those *happenings*, together with the shock of the spider,' she shuddered, 'shifted the energy and cleared the air and my head. It's all quite magical, Ronnie, don't you think?'

'If you say so, Mum,' said Ronnie grabbing the brandy and putting it away.

'So maybe a few words of empowerment, an enchantment or two, may just push events along and who knows? Maybe…' Minerva's wistful gaze drifted out of the window to the garden.

'Do you mean a man, by any chance, mother? I think in all possibility, *he* could be on the cards for a change, don't you?'

'You could be right, dear.' Minerva cleared her throat. 'I never thought I'd say it…but the time has come to get to work.'

* * *

When Isis rang the Crafty Cottage doorbell later that day, she was fit to burst. The memory of what had passed only minutes before danced about in her mind and all over her face. Brimming with excitement, she hopped from one leg to the other, barely able to contain herself. After what seemed like an age, a dishevelled looking Minerva appeared.

'Isis…aren't you a little early for our class? I thought it was seven.' She glanced at the clock in the hallway. 'And it's only five.'

'I know that, Minerva; I'm just passing on my way back from the shop…but I *had* to stop and let you know…' She glanced over her shoulder.

'Shut the door behind you please,' Minerva called from the kitchen, putting the kettle on.

Firmly planted in the living room and waiting for her friend to join her, Isis pondered over the past few months. The belly- dancing classes had been the best thing for both of them, especially after she had lost her husband Derek to the Molly Maid of all things and Minerva had lost her friend Eve to that awful illness. Joining the class had proved a real tonic and they had bonded right from the start. And what a scream it was! The perfect excuse (and remedy for her lack of confidence) for Isis to indulge in her Egyptian fetish.

Changing her name had felt entirely natural and seemed to seal her fate with the hallmark of mystery and magic. Isis – Egyptian Goddess. It was far better than plain old Beryl and she *felt* so different, too; nothing like the dowdy, boring woman she had begun to think she looked and felt like. Minerva was right, it had transformed her.

It was the best thing she'd ever done and now she was never out of her dancing attire. In fact, she wore it all the time. Such wonderful colours and exquisite materials, the silks, the satins and the sandals. Oh, and the hair-pieces, how she loved them...so glamorous. Admittedly, she was still learning to get it right and some of them *did* keel to one side slightly, but the point was she was daring to be different, she was taking the plunge. Shedding her old skin (just like snakes did, as Minerva put it) had never felt better.

Minerva swanned into the room with renewed vigour and two steaming mugs. 'Right then, out with it, Isis.'

'Well...I was at the shop and noticed a poster on the board outside...' She paused.

Minerva took a deep breath. 'And? Anything interesting?'

She shuffled in her chair, noticing that the angle of her friend's hair- piece was not quite as acute as it usually was. She was pleased to see that practise was making a little nearer to perfect. It was a progress of sorts.

'Well...'

'Will you spit it out, Isis, before I give up the will to live?'

'We have a new vicar.'

Minerva looked at her friend and felt the old stirrings of contempt in the pit of her stomach.

'A new vicar?' She sneered. 'Well, I suppose it's about time. Though the village has been without one for six months now and nobody seems to have suffered too much. The church is still standing and so are the people.'

Sarcasm came easily to Minerva when it came to matters of a religious nature, especially with regard to the Christian faith. Not that it was a bad one or that she had anything against any Christians personally but she felt, as a Pagan and practicing Witch (and proud of it), that the church had an awful lot to answer for. Somewhere buried deep in her subconscious lurked the collective memories of those poor souls who'd suffered for only ever being different from the church, for daring to resist and turn away from the power that sought to dominate and control the masses.

Those poor victims of corruption.

All those innocent people, branded 'heretics' and 'devil-worshippers', just because they didn't need a priest or a vicar or someone who was ordained to act as an intermediary between them and the creative forces of the world.

Crimes against humanity she could not endure or forgive any man for. Shame on them! It was more than enough to get her started and step right up there onto her worn and battered soap-box.

'He's gorgeous, Minerva.'

'How do you know?'

'He was in the shop.'

'Married?'

'Not sure,' said Isis.

'There's only one way to find out, then,' said Minerva.

'By doing what?'

'Going to church, of course. When's his first gig?'

'Gig?' Isis looked puzzled.

'Yes, his first performance.' Minerva flung out her arms. 'The pulpit is the perfect stage for a new vicar.'

Sometimes, thought Minerva, Isis fell just a little too far behind.

And sometimes, thought Isis, Minerva was a little too forward for her own good.

* * *

The two friends settled down nicely with their second Brazilian no.5 coffee and were munching on a combination of Bombay mix and jammie dodgers. Cupboard contents, according to Minerva, were for making do to a greater or lesser extent, depending on the situation. Going with the flow was most important and she really did try to walk her talk...most of the time.

'Funny you should say that, Minerva,' said Isis, with a mouthful of Bombay mix and biscuit.

'Say what, Isis?' said Minerva with thoughts of pulpits and preachers filling her mind.

'About his 'gig'...you know...the vicar.'

As if she needed reminding.

'Oh yes that...and *him*,' said Minerva. 'What about it?'

'Well, he plays the *guitar*, of all things. He was carrying one in a case in the shop and on the poster it says 'a social evening of Faith and Fun, accompanied by the vicar and his..."

'... Instrument?'

'Well, yes...I suppose so... Minerva, stop it!'

'Isis, really! I was referring to his guitar, of course.'

'Minerva, it might help to drag yourself out of the gutter and actually take on board what this means.'

'Sometimes, Isis, a bit of gutter humour is *exactly* what's needed. After all, it's the salt of the earth, don't you think? Without it, we're an unsavoury bunch. Anyway...what in heaven's name *does* it mean?'

She felt slightly giddy in the suddenly odd and almost celestial atmosphere.

'Well...it means we have within our midst a man of the cloth who is not only dishy, but possibly unmarried and relatively modern as well as musical...'

'He might have a girlfriend.'

'Vicars are not the kind of people who have girlfriends, are they?'

'Yes, I know what you mean,' said Minerva. 'They're either married or celibate these *cloth men.*'

'Or closet homosexuals.'

Minerva clutched her mouth after spitting out a mouthful of soggy Bombay mix.

'Steady on,' said Isis and patted her friend hard on the back. 'Thanks,' croaked Minerva. 'Does he look like a 'closet cloth man', do you think?'

Isis thought for a moment. 'Well, having never really known one or at least not one that I was aware of...I can't say.'

Minerva couldn't help but be moved by the endearing honesty of her friend, as peculiar as it was at times like these.

'Looks like we're going to have to find out.' Minerva slapped the coffee table hard, sending Bombay mix flying into the jammie dodgers. 'I feel an *inspection* in the air, Isis. When is this so-called social gathering of Faith and Fun? Not sure that I'd put those two words together in a Christian sentence, but I suppose anything goes these days.'

'I think it's this Saturday, 7.30 pm, at the church.'

'Any refreshments? I mean, other than the usual tea and coffee, jam and Jerusalem?'

'You're thinking W.I.'

'No, I'm thinking brandy… Shall we chance the possibility that in this new man of the cloth's thoroughly modern and musical mind there is space for the inclusion of alcohol on the church refreshment list – or not? In which case, I will take my own, discreetly carried upon my person, of course.'

Isis glared at her. 'Will that be necessary?'

She knew only too well that it would be. Minerva did nothing by halves.

'Oh, absolutely it will. But then again…we don't want to give the wrong impression now, do we?'

Isis prodded her hair-piece and glared at Minerva.

'No,' she said, 'we don't.'

4

The Hermit and the Thin Blue Line

Ronnie came out of hiding at last. After her mother's early morning antics in the garden, her bedroom had provided a much needed bolt-hole. Thanks to a good sleep, the pounding head had gone, but she still had that horrible, nauseous feeling, and remembered she hadn't eaten since the day before.

Within seconds of leaving her bed, she rushed to the bathroom to hug the toilet bowl. Why did she do this to herself? It had to be the drink. She'd overdone it on the Druid Fluid last night. It was a perfectly reasonable explanation. But hadn't she forgotten something? The packet in her bag loomed into her mind and she pushed it as far back as she could. Needing a distraction and after making a feeble attempt to tidy herself up, she followed the sound of voices coming from the front room downstairs.

Minerva looked up at her daughter. 'Hello darling! Didn't hear the front door go. Have you been in long?'

'I didn't go in...'

Minerva frowned at her.

'I didn't feel well enough,' whined Ronnie. 'Besides, I'm well up to speed with the work, Mum. Don't fret. I didn't have any lectures today.'

'Okay, but what about Bob?'

College was one thing, her horse was another.

'Sophia said she'd feed him and turn him out for me. I'm going to pop down there now and get him in. The fresh air and a bike ride will do me good.'

Minerva was unconvinced. 'What's the matter, Ron? You look dreadfully pale. Anything you've eaten?'

Ronnie looked sheepishly at her mother. 'A bit too much cider last night, I suppose.'

'Rhiannon! I take back all sympathy.'

That's rich, coming from you, thought Ronnie.

Minerva glared at her daughter. 'Sometimes I wonder about you. You're eighteen, for heaven's sake and old enough to be showing responsibility, if not for yourself, then for your horse!'

'All right, Mum...don't go on...please.' *I might just be pregnant and how am I going to tell you that?*

'Do you want any dinner later? I'll leave it in the oven.'

'Yes, please, I might feel like it by then,' said Ronnie. 'Where are you off to?'

'Belly dancing tonight.' Minerva looked at Isis and thrust her chest out and up into a Turkish clinch. 'Really getting the hang of it now aren't we, Ice?'

Ronnie finally spotted Isis, tucked at the end of the sofa. 'Isis! I didn't see you there for a moment...sorry!'

'That's quite all right, Ronnie...it's allowed.' Isis winked at her. 'Just been filling your mother in on the latest village *news.*' She looked at Minerva and back at Ronnie. 'We have a new vicar in the parish.'

'Oh...' said Ronnie, '... and?'

'*Apparently*,' said Minerva, 'he's single...we think. Sexuality to be confirmed.' She glanced at Isis. 'He plays the guitar in church *and* he's gorgeous! I'd say that's incentive enough for the pursuit of all things un-trivial, wouldn't you?'

Oh God, thought Ronnie. 'Which one's going for him, then?' She made her way out into the hallway. 'Looks like a heads-or-tails job for you two!'

An uncomfortable silence hovered between Minerva and Isis as the front door slammed behind Ronnie...leaving a crimson faced Isis frantically plumping up the cushions on the sofa.

'He'll probably go for you, Minerva, you're...far more attractive and...well...you've more confidence than me. Anyway, I could do with a bit more time to get over Derek.'

'Oh, how very sweet of you, Ice, but let's not get ahead of ourselves. I haven't even *seen* him yet and you've no idea what he's really like either. He may well be into...' she paused, '... the more genteel type. One never knows; neither should one assume *anything* until all has been revealed, *especially* his sexual preferences.'

'No, you're right, Minerva.' 'Meanwhile, we have work to do.' 'Spell time?'

'Dare I say it, Ice; I feel it's under way already!' Isis looked puzzled. 'What have you started?'

'I had one of those awful migraines this morning and experienced a clearing of the cobwebs, one might say. It was all wonderfully magical and enlightening and, to add to it, I'd decided to work a spell to help things on their way...to attract a man, is what I had in mind. I think it's about time: a girl can only mope after a wander-lusting husband for so long.'

Thank goodness for that, thought Isis. She'd come to her senses at last.

'Well, you're always saying how powerful the mind is, Minerva, and how the work begins as soon as it's thought about.'

Isis was learning fast. As soon as magic crept into the conversation, Minerva could literally feel it all around her; sparkling about the hemisphere and permeating every orifice. Nothing was more exciting.

'How right you are, Isis. Our thoughts do indeed kick-start the process, but then we *have* to propel it along with the right ingredients...nothing is more powerful than the fuel of our own emotions.'

She was reaching for a huge hardback off the book shelf where books were crammed in their masses from end to end. The towering oak case creaked towards her as she wrenched the one she wanted away from all the others.

There were books on herbs, books on crystals, books on angels, books on Gods and Goddesses, books on mythology, books on astrology, books on philosophy and psychology; books, in fact, on every metaphysical subject you could think of.

However, the overwhelming majority were her books on magic. These were her points of reference she returned to again and again. One lifetime would never be enough to extract all the juice, as far as Minerva was concerned. She opened out the great book and dived excitedly between the pages...

You can't separate a Witch from her spell book, thought Isis.

'Ah, here it is,' said Minerva. 'Juniper berries...I thought so.'

'What for?' asked Isis.

'*Juniper berries possess tremendous love-drawing and sexuality-enhancing powers...* This is what we want, Ice...' Minerva straightened her glasses, '*Juniper Spell for Seeking New Love...*

49

Hot Mama Douche? I think we'll skip that – sounds far too messy, not to mention smelly… Vinegar, of all things! I don't think so, do you?' Minerva screwed up her nose.

'Doesn't bear thinking about,' said Isis. 'To douche or not to douche…?'

'…is definitely *not* the question,' finished Minerva.

'What's spell number two? Read on…' said Isis.

'Well, the vinegar's still in it, but perhaps not quite as…*intrusively*, shall we say?'

'So, what do you do?'

Isis let out a long sigh while Minerva cleared her throat:

'*Number one: Soak the juniper berries in vinegar for several hours. Two: Strain out the berries, reserving some and adding a generous quantity of the infusion to your bath water…*'

'…Again?'

'What do you mean, 'again'? This is a bath, not the douche thing!'

'Isn't it the same?'

Minerva ignored her and carried on:

'*Three: Enjoy your bath while visualizing a successful love match. Four: Emerge from bath and toss the bathwater and reserved berries outside, on to the earth near your home, to signal your desire for love.*'

'That will take some doing,' said Isis. 'I like a nice, full bath, right to the top.'

'The sign of a good spell, Isis, is when you have to work at it. It isn't worth doing unless you put some effort into it. That's when the power takes effect.'

'Yes, Minerva, so you keep telling me, but really… Does it mean toss out *all* the bathwater, or do you think one could get away with a token toss?'

Minerva peered over her glasses at Isis.

'I'm sure in your case, Isis, that would be fine. As for myself, I shall go the whole hog and work on a full toss, as I like to do things properly. It could make all the difference, you know. But here...' She drew the book closer. 'This might be more up your street...the *Easy Juniper Spell* says that all you need to do is: *Pierce, string and wear the berries on one's person to attract a lover.*'

'Now, that sounds more like it,' said Isis to Minerva, hovering behind the battered book spine. 'So now to find a juniper tree...or is it a bush?'

'Does it matter?' said Minerva, chewing her lip. 'I'm pretty sure they grow over the graveyard. Shall we go and have a look before class?'

Isis jumped up from the sofa. 'I'll be back later for berry picking and belly dancing, in that order.'

'Sounds like a plan.' Minerva smiled, and picking a tarot card, placed it between the pages of her book. 'I can hardly wait to get started,' she said to the bright, pulsating colours of the Fool, as she showed her friend out.

* * *

The next morning, a thin blue line stared back at Ronnie, as she hunched over the sink holding onto its side for support. Did she really think she was going to get away with it? Her mind swayed from one thought to another. Round and round it went, in a circle of confusion and fragments of hazy scenes and images, of faces and sounds and smells and the touch of skin on skin and the urgent fumblings of a shameless, primal instinct.

She remembered a strange sort of pleasure, almost over before it had started in a pull and a push, in a shake of the head and a cry of crude abandon. It stirred a dizzy sensation that she'd soon forgotten and pushed back as far back as it would go.

But it came back. Her mind raced with people and places, spinning round in a spiral with no direction and it brought up a feeling inside like she'd never known. It threatened and clawed and crawled up on the inside. Alien thoughts turned to feelings and surged through her and pushed and shoved and circled until they came up in a torrent of liquid and tears.

She felt better afterwards and dressed quickly, making her way down the stairs, careful not to wake her mother, as it was still early. At the bottom of the stairs was Lucifer, cracking the bones of some poor animal and wolfing down the contents. This was a normal morning ritual of his and she blamed the cat flap for letting it happen.

As she jumped over the munching cat, he carried on feasting without looking up once. Cats are like that: totally in their own world, drifting over to the world of humans only when it suits them. But mostly it doesn't. Cats like to suit themselves, and the black moggy of Crafty Cottage was no exception.

'Oh lovely… What have you got this time, Luce?' Ronnie wrinkled her nose as she grabbed her jacket and boots.

The cat carried on regardless. It was breakfast time, after all.

* * *

At the sight of his mistress wobbling up the path on her bike, Bob Marley called out his hello. A soft whinny and a nod of shaggy forelock were enough to melt any girl's heart, especially a girl who was out of sorts. A blast along the sea wall should do it, thought Ronnie: the perfect remedy. She was far too busy with her thoughts to notice the farrier's van parked around the corner in the main yard, or the tell-tale wafts of smoke sailing downwind.

Stable duties done, Ronnie strolled over to the nearby field gate for a much needed cigarette. With each deep inhalation – instead of making her feel worse – it surprised her to find it settled the fluttering in her stomach. She looked out across the field and noticed the sky around her. The dark clouds hung in curtains over a glimpse of pale blue. What a big and beautiful picture the universe paints, she thought. As she gazed around her, she felt small in comparison and mused over the idea. Everything must be relative…and there must be more to life. Lost in her daydream, she didn't hear the crunch of the gravel behind her, or the cough.

'All right, Ron?'

She turned round to see Gavin, as bold as brass…in the flesh, there in front of her. What the hell did he want?

'Gavin… How are you?'

A fleeting moment of passion is all it was.

'Yeah, all right, thanks. What about you? Haven't seen you for a while, not since the…party.' At least he had the decency to look embarrassed.

'Oh, busy with college and stuff, you know… Lots of painting to do. Got my portfolio to fill up…' She dropped the cigarette and Gavin trod on it.

'Didn't know you smoked?'

'No, I gave up.'

'Feeling a bit stressed?' The question made her feel awkward.

'Maybe…' she laughed nervously. 'Yeah, you could say that.'

'I'm sure it's nothing you can't handle.'

If only you knew.

'If you fancy a drink some time, a bit of a de-stressor… If you're up for it, that is?'

She'd forgotten what a nice smile he had. 'Some time, maybe… I'd like that, yeah.'

What was she saying?

He was tapping madly at his mobile. 'What's your number?'

She gave it to him. *This is madness!*

He shuffled from one boot to another, staring at the ground. 'Look… Ronnie…about the party, I'm sorry if I was a bit full on with you… The drink an' all that…'

'Yeah, bloody drink!' she laughed. 'I'd had a skinful, too…happens to us all, Gavin. Not to worry, eh?'

'Yeah, just wanted to apologise, that's all,' he said. 'I like you, Ron, and I wouldn't want you getting the wrong impression.'

Oh, really…what impression would that be? When did a roll in the hay become not a roll in the hay? Now she was more confused than ever. Did she like him or didn't she? She wanted to scream.

'We all make mistakes, and…' She stared hard at the gatepost.

'Yeah, but it wasn't…a mistake. It's just that… Oh, I don't know what I'm trying to say.'

Neither do I, thought Ronnie, *but whatever it is, you're making a good job of digging a great big hole for yourself, and I'm not falling in it with you.*

He was turning her off like a tap. Fast.

She had never been more grateful for the sound of Bob banging at his stable door. He wanted to go out as much as she did.

'Look, Gavin, got to go… Bob's getting impatient. See you later…'

Don't ask me when. Don't ask me when.

'Righto, Ronnie. I'll be in touch...if that's okay?'

'See ya, Gavin.' She marched towards the stables, trying not to wonder what kind of a weird thing had just gone on between them. She didn't see Gavin shrugging his shoulders heavily as he walked off.

Maybe they were both confused. But she didn't need it. She didn't need *him*. That much was clear to her, and for that she was grateful. By process of elimination and realizing what she didn't want, she'd get closer to what she *did* want. Right?

Mum's words of wisdom again. Maybe it was *her mother* she should speak to? No, perhaps not. Not at the moment. It could wait; she had better things to do.

Burning some turf with Bob was one of them.

* * *

The clouds soon cleared and she found herself pounding hard along the sea wall under a canopy of turquoise. She never tired of this stretch of land, and neither did Bob.

Boudicca screamed through her veins, her warhorse rippled beneath her and together they charged like warriors into battle. The earthiness of the damp fields mingled with the salt of the sea, filling her lungs in a cold rush and stinging her cheeks. The mighty hand of the God of air reached down and slapped her hard, until the tears came and dried before they fell.

Perhaps if I go fast enough, thought Ronnie, *and ride hard enough, maybe it could change this situation, turn it all around. Maybe it'll clear things up and I won't have to think about it. I won't have to decide and I won't have to live with any regrets.*

If she made something happen now, would she regret that?

Or would she regret it not happening? Which one?

If it was possible for thoughts to travel that fast around her mind, then it was possible to make a decision just as fast, but all roads led to nowhere. She only knew that this was the best way at the moment...pounding the earth on horseback.

Bob's breathing began to labour and the steam rose from his body. It was just like a natural sauna, thought Ronnie. She'd been riding hard for a couple of miles and the moving scenery had passed in a never ending blur, along with the tangled thoughts in her mind.

Horse and rider eventually pulled up and slowed down into a steady walk, the sea wall still stretching miles ahead of them. She realised her thoughts had not gone anywhere; the gallop had just numbed them. They hovered round the edges of her mind, refusing to budge.

Nothing was working.

Then she saw it. At first she couldn't make out what it was through the rising steam. But, as they got nearer, the shape took form, growing in size and build until they were almost upon it. Wispy strands of ethereal mist surrounded it and she sensed the density of her body lighten as they approached. Whatever it was posed no threat to Bob, as he seemed unnaturally calm in its presence.

Ronnie squeezed her fingers on the reins and sat completely still, hardly breathing, eyes fixed on the figure ahead. The tall man, dressed in a long, dark cloak, seemed familiar, somehow. His head was bowed and hidden under a hood. Leaning heavily on a tall stick with one hand, he carried a lantern in the other.

Then it came to her...her mother's tarot. What a memorable upbringing with the magical cards she'd had. Each character had become an extended member of the family and she couldn't ignore the colourful influence they'd had on her life. And here was the sage of the deck, the Hermit, right in front of her...

The mystical figure seemed totally unaware of Boudicca and her warhorse, but looked out to the fields, beyond the worn track of the sea wall and into the distance.

Bob wrinkled his muzzle and stomped the ground in a horsey salute as the Hermit turned to face them.

'Ahh...there you are, Travellers. I've been waiting for you. Time to rest awhile and renew your energy.'

He gestured to the ground and Ronnie slipped down and stood beside Bob, not quite believing what she was seeing, hearing or doing.

'You have some soul-searching to do, young Traveller,' he continued. 'I think you know that. And you're wondering how I do...'

'Well...I'm not...sure,' she mumbled. 'Who *are* you?'

'I think you know that also, and yet cannot bring yourself to believe that it may be true...that I might just be who you think I am. Will you take that leap of faith? Will you recognize in me that which is for your highest good, that which has come to guide you at this time?'

'You *are* the Hermit, then?' There...she'd said it.

He smiled and spoke softly: 'So you *do* recognize me? That's good! We can work together to untangle the knots that bind you, to lift the shadow that has cast itself over you and make sense of what is happening. But first, a time of rest. Be patient with yourself and do not allow the mind to fret and agitate. Like a dog with a bone, the time has come to let it go. The troubled waters must quieten and become like the millpond. Only when all is calm, will you begin to see with clarity.'

His words struck a chord deep within Ronnie and silenced

her with a feeling of peace she had never known before. She stood mesmerized, while Bob hung his head and casually rested a back leg. A calm horse is a peaceful one.

'I will bid you farewell and visit again as time unfolds, young Traveller. Meanwhile, turn within and invoke me, if you need to. My mind is always available to you.'

His parting words seemed to change something in Ronnie. Gone was the heavy burden she had carried before and, turning to where the Hermit had stood, she noticed he had gone, too. She was surprised only with herself, perhaps, for accepting the incident without question. But did it matter? As far as she was concerned, it had been a perfectly natural occurrence, touching her with a bit of magic. No words could do it justice and no justification was needed. It was between her and Bob...and the Hermit.

A very different Boudicca reached for the stirrup and sprang back onto her horse, and the warriors headed for home.

The battle was over...for the time being.

5

Juniper Berries and the Vicar

Graveyards are not the best-lit of places, especially at night. Seeing in the dark is not easy and appearances can be deceptive. This was something Minerva and Isis had not anticipated as they surveyed the contents of their graveyard pickings from the night before.

'It said *juniper* berries, Minerva. Are you sure that's what these are?' asked Isis, inspecting the berries sprawled out on Minerva's kitchen table.

'I would certainly like to think so, Isis.'

'It's no good just thinking so, Minerva: you have to *know* so.'

'Now, just a minute, Isis...we spent nearly an hour in that graveyard – in the dark, I might add – picking these things against all odds!'

'Exactly, Minerva! It was dark and it's easy to make mistakes when you can't see what you're doing. You must admit, we weren't entirely sure we'd got the right tree...or bush, or whatever it was.' Isis twiddled her hair-piece fiercely.

'Then why didn't you say at the time? We could have saved ourselves the job.'

'But that's my point. We didn't really have the time to spare, did we? As it was, we were late for our belly dancing class.'

Minerva picked up one of the squishy, red berries and peered closely at it. 'Are you saying these are *not* juniper berries? I thought we'd agreed they were.'

'No! I mean, yes, well... I think it was more like *you* were certain they were... I had my reservations.'

'Oh, I do wish you'd pipe up and *voice* your reservations, Isis,' said Minerva. 'Fortune favours the bold, you know.'

Easy for you to say, thought Isis. 'I've just got a feeling those red berries are not juniper. In fact, I'm almost certain juniper berries are *blue*.'

Minerva looked at the mass of velvety berries oozing red juice all over the table. 'So if these are *not* the precious juniper berries, what are they?'

'I think they're *yew* berries,' proclaimed Isis. 'And, if they are, they're extremely poisonous and *not* something that should be sitting on your kitchen table.'

'Or staining it.' Minerva frowned. 'Are you sure?'

'Not entirely,' said Isis, 'But I don't think it's worth taking the chance, do you?' She looked up to see the horror on Minerva's face. 'We don't want to jeopardize a good spell now, do we?'

No we certainly don't, thought Minerva. She liked to believe she was past making mistakes, but one could never be sure. It reminded her of the time she had made a healing pouch for her mother, who was suffering with painful arthritis. She had stuffed the pouch full of herbs and one with rather a strong smell that she had ignored at the time. But all was revealed when her mother had rung to say her pain had gone and so had her nasal hairs...and should she have sniffed the stuff quite so hard? Only on later inspection of the herb, did Minerva discover the leaves of the aggressively odorous curry plant she had mistaken for the thyme it should have been. Not the best of ingredients to add to her list of successful spells and consequently she never added it again. Neither did she tell her mother. It seemed unnecessary – and, as far as she was concerned, the spell had worked somehow and that was an end to it.

But one could never be too careful.

'Jeopardize a good spell? No, Isis... That is definitely something we do *not* want to do.'

'Right then,' said Isis, 'that's sorted, then.'

Minerva began rounding up the half-squashed berries and scooping them into the bin.

'So, where do we get juniper berries then, Isis, if not from the graveyard?'

'I think you'll find a health food shop should have them, with a bit of luck.'

'Well as you know, I don't believe in *luck,*' snorted Minerva. 'It's all about being in the right place at the right time.'

'You mean synchronicity?'

'Now you're talking! I shall take a road trip in Mr. Morris, in search of the elusive berries... Clearly a spell worth working a little harder at, don't you think?'

'And isn't that the sign of a good one? It's what you're always telling me,' said Isis.

'Ah yes...then it must be true,' said Minerva, grabbing her car keys.

Isis followed her to the front door. 'You'll be needing this...' she said, handing Minerva her bag and smoothing out her own bright green wrap-around skirt on the way.
Satin did have an awful habit of creasing.

* * *

Ronnie blew the straying wisps of hair away from her face with short puffs of breath. She smiled as Bob joined in with a series of snorts and they puffed and snorted their way back to the yard in perfect harmony. She wondered if it had all been a dream. Meeting the Hermit wasn't exactly an everyday occurrence was it? What would her mother say? Maybe she'd tell her after the *other thing*, although she didn't feel quite as fretful about it since the Hermit's appearance.

Somehow, she knew it was pointless worrying. What good did that ever do? No… She would take heed of his wise words and let go of that bone for now. Worrying was a tiring and useless pastime. He'd told her to rest and be patient and the more she thought about it, the more sense it made to her muddled mind.

It was quite amazing how different she felt.

Bob seemed more chilled-out, too. Although usually a laid-back sort of chap, he was not insensitive to his rider's edginess of late. Her jangled nerves may not have been quite so obvious to some people, but did not escape his keen senses. In fact a troubled mistress was enough to provoke any empathy a horse could have; strengthening the bond between them.

Ronnie dismounted and walked alongside her horse as they approached the yard. She rubbed his mane and breathed in the strong, earthy aroma oozing from every pore of his being.

'Don't know what I'd do without you, old boy,' she said, wrapping an arm around his neck. 'We're good together, you and me.'

He flicked an ear back towards the voice he knew so well, pulled the reins forwards and nodded in agreement. Ronnie laughed and stopped suddenly at the dull thud of a bird's wings overhead. She looked up to see a barn owl swooping past them, low to the ground, heading for the trees beyond.

'That's got to be an omen, Bob.' She had no idea what it could mean, but felt it must be significant in some way. Time would tell, no doubt. She was reminded of her mother, who loved owls with a passion. She said they were symbols of all-knowing and the awakening of psychic power. She said they were the watchers of the skies and the wisdom keepers of secret knowledge, of the mysteries.
She said they were magical beings.

At that moment, her mother was the only person Ronnie wanted to see, and she quickened her stride. She was ready to tell her secret. It wouldn't be easy, but this was her mother after all, and they were close.

How hard could it be?

* * *

Minerva was not in the mood. Not for yew berries that should have been juniper berries, not for any kind of spell assembling or casting, not for cold or *hot* callers. She was closed for business. Would she ever get used to these plummets and swings? There was never any warning. No smoke signal or jungle drum to herald the arrival of the hormonal brigade as they wobbled and thundered down the highway from hell and gate-crashed into her system. Some women sailed through it, comfortably cruising along the calm waters of their menopausal millpond without so much as a ripple. *Well, bully for them*, thought Minerva.

They were the fortunate ones.

She was, undoubtedly, not one of those, but more of a young, warrior Crone who soldiered on through the sometimes terrifying and maddening battles of the weirdest war she had ever known. She was one of those who found themselves teetering on the edge of a life raft, reduced to a single plank, worn down by the raging and treacherous currents of an unpredictable and undulating sea of wretched emotions. She was one of those who, upon reaching her middle years, found herself the owner of a colourful vocabulary with a mind of its own. She was one of those who didn't believe in innocent people – because everyone was guilty of something.

In fact, she was one of those women who – when the mood was upon them – would find something wrong with almost anything. It's what they were programmed to do…and by their hormones, of course. The blighters were rampant and running wild ever since the day of their coronation – crowned rulers of the men-o-whats-it kingdom.

'Off with your bloody heads, YOU BASTARDS!' yelled Minerva. She found a good yell did wonders to soothe the menopausal brow, particularly in the early stages of a hot flush.

She'd been in a shop once, when sensing the ferocity of an attack, she'd had the urge to strip off on the spot. She managed to remedy the situation by rushing out on to a busy high street in mid-purchase to get some air. The puzzled shop assistant chased after Minerva and found her crumpled in a burning heap on the metal dustbin outside. It had been the nearest resting place although not the best choice on a summer's day; she could still smell it now.

Fortunately, she had already paid for the 'chakra bouncing' DVD and left it on the counter without thinking. But, thanks to the quick-thinking shop assistant, all was not lost. What made it interesting was that he was straddling a space hopper at the time. She had wondered if the demonstration in the shop was a little over ambitious, but the young man was a confident sort, leap-frogging her and the bin before crashing into some poor old lady on a disabled buggy. It wasn't a pretty sight and the kind of experience that had burned itself into Minerva's memory, scarring her for life.

No, hot flushes were not for the faint-hearted.

* * *

Ronnie returned home to a fanfare of music blaring from every open window in the house – which happened to be all of them. Under the circumstances, she wasn't up to the throbbing pulse of heavy calypso, but she knew the signs only too well. Mother was under the influence of one of those mad flushes. Typical.

At times like these, Lucifer disappeared for at least a whole day and night, tolerating neither voices or music at high volume. Ronnie imagined he escaped to the peace and quiet of a good old rat-infested ditch or an empty barn, where there was sure to be another farm cat and the latest battle of claws would ensue. He usually returned in the next few days, a shadowy figure of his former self, looking for food and sympathy.

Why, thought Ronnie, *does one of Mother's flushes have to be now?* She wondered about sneaking off until things had cooled down, but didn't have the energy to work out where to go. She would face the music and face her mother, whatever state she was in. She probably wouldn't even notice her.

There was only one way to find out.

* * *

Driven by these surges of fired-up emotion, Minerva had discovered that the best way of dealing with them was to dance it out of her system. What better way than to climb aboard the tidal wave and ride it? Stripping down to bare essentials, she cavorted from room to room in sheer, unashamed abandonment when the front door opened.

Ronnie was used to her mother's frantic habits and normally took it all in her stride. She was tentatively working her way through the hall when Minerva careered from the living room like a mad octopus, arms and legs and hair everywhere.
She looks like she's been plugged into the national grid, thought Ronnie.

'Hi, Mum!' she shouted, above the thumping bass.

Minerva waved frantically. 'Hello, darling!' she mouthed in mid-gyration, spiralling around Ronnie in a frenzy. And when the music stopped suddenly, so did Minerva, hanging off the banister like a rag doll.

'Mum, why have you got my shorts on?' asked Ronnie, not unkindly. 'Those are my best ones.'

Minerva glanced down at the shorts in surprise. 'Oh, darling, I never really noticed. I just grabbed the nearest thing in the airing cupboard that looked like it would cover as little of me as possible. You know how these awful flushes affect me,' she panted. 'It's the only way I can get through it.'

'I wouldn't mind, Mum, but they don't really fit, do they?' Ronnie nodded to the gaping flies and bulging buttonhole in front of her.

'Sorry, darling, but with a bit of luck I'll have lost a few pounds. Wonderful for the figure, you know, and I've been dancing for a good hour! You don't know how lucky you are, at your age. Make the most of your maidenhood!'

Does she know? thought Ronnie.

'Do you want a cuppa, Mum?' she called from the kitchen. 'Good idea, love. Better make it a herbal, though, don't want to push these adrenals any more than necessary…'

'You look like you could do with a rest,' Ronnie called from the kitchen, biting her lip as the hot water splashed into the cups. They retired to the living room with herbal refreshment and jammie dodgers to satisfy the growing rumbles in Ronnie's stomach. Minerva looked across at her daughter's pasty complexion as she tucked ravenously into the biscuits. 'What is it, darling?'

Maybe this won't be so hard, thought Ronnie, Mum is psychic, after all.

'Where are your cards, Mum?' she asked, scanning the room. Minerva's tarot were never far away.

'You'll find them by the phone, Ron. I was about to make a start on the 'lines' earlier, before falling prey to the flush from hell.'

Ronnie managed a weak smile, then picked up the cards and waited while her mother cleared a space on the coffee table and lit a candle. Minerva took her spiritual work seriously and creating the right atmosphere was crucial. She reached for a large chunk of labradorite, her favourite crystal, and placed it next to the candle. At the flick of a nearby switch, the angelic ripples of a Celtic harp filtered out into the room, transporting them to the celestial spheres. Apprehension hung in the air as Ronnie sent out her plea of help to the universe and Minerva connected to her own guiding forces.

'Do you have a question?' she asked.

Ronnie nodded. She didn't need to say it and Minerva didn't need to know. It was better if she didn't, as the cards would reveal the answers; they always did.

'Okay, we'll just do a simple three-card spread then,' said Minerva, handing the cards to Ronnie. 'Give them a good shuffle and don't look so nervous.'

Ronnie picked her cards and waited while her mother took in her first impression.

'Okay,' said Minerva slowly. 'We have the Ten of Pentacles...the Six of Pentacles...and the Five of Swords...'

She smoothed both her hands along the edge of the table and leaned closer to the cards, almost smelling them. 'Well, the numbers alone suggest a situation where there is possibly one too many and, although it has the capacity to bring harmony and balance, it also raises challenges, whatever it is...' She peered up at her daughter.

Ronnie tingled. How did she manage to get so close so quickly?

Minerva cleared her throat. 'Then we have Pentacles, indicating family matters with the Ten and sharing with the Six...finishing up with the Five of Swords. Yes, definitely a fear that needs facing, but it's a real challenge, whatever it is. Therefore...taking all the dynamics into account, it seems we have an over-flowing family problem that needs to be talked about. It's pretty serious by the look and feel of it...making sense?' She looked at her ashen-faced daughter.

Ronnie couldn't move. Her body was rigid with the fear her mother had described and she felt sick... It gnawed deep in her belly, wrenching the muscles over in slow twists. She wanted to get up and run, but she couldn't. She wanted to hide and not come out. She wanted to climb out of the black hole that threatened to suck her down into its bottomless pit, but she was stuck and she was scared.

The tears spilled fast and Ronnie looked down at her hands contorting like snakes around themselves and she tried to speak, to say something...but nothing came. She had no words. They were lost before they formed...like the life inside her.

Her chest heaved and she was helpless against the cry as it came. The front of her body caved inwards, just as her mother's arms went around her. 'It's all right, Ron, it's all right.' Minerva held on to her as she cried.

Ronnie clung to the one person – apart from her father – who would not judge her, who loved her unconditionally. She knew that, without question, whatever she had done, whatever happened, she could trust her mother. Nothing could ever be so bad that she could not tell her. Minerva had told her this many times over the years, and she had never had any reason to doubt it. It had made all the difference before and still did now. It had been the difference between her sticking around and running away. The difference between a mess and something that could be sorted out. The difference between a happy ending and a nightmare. The difference between life and death now, perhaps.

Minerva was the first to pull away. Keeping both hands on her daughter's shoulders, she stared straight at her. 'Pregnant... Am I right?'

Ronnie shot her a wounded look.

'Are you going to tell me or do you want a thousand questions?' Minerva squeezed her shoulders.

No, Ronnie didn't want that. Turning around and leaning back into her mother's arms, she took a deep breath in... 'It was the stables' party. Gavin, the farrier guy... We'd both had a lot to drink and...' She looked at her mother. 'It was a mistake! I don't even...like him that much, not really. I was a bit upset beforehand...'

'What about?'

'Joe. I'd seen him with a girl...some posh bird...a boat owner's daughter.'

'Joe?'

'Yes... *Joe*, Mum! I didn't realise I liked him...not in that way...until then. So I went to a party, got smashed and had a one night stand... I *know* it was stupid! I wasn't thinking... I didn't think that I...that *this* would happen!'

'Does...Gavin know? Have you told him?' Minerva took her hands from Ronnie's shoulders and folded them in her lap.

'God, no! I've only just found out myself... Mum,' she pleaded, 'please don't say anything...to anyone...not yet.'

'Of course I won't! So you've done a test...how many weeks?' She knew how sophisticated the kits were these days.

'Five... I think.'

'Then you must go and have a chat with the doctor and we'll take it from there.' Minerva's matter-of-fact tone was reassuring and Ronnie felt a wave of relief.

This was a little too close to home for Minerva. A painful reminder, history repeating itself. Oh, the irony! This had been Ronnie's way into the world...a gift from heaven, wrapped up in guilt and regret. Her beautiful mistake. She'd never told anyone, not even Ronnie.

Minerva was grateful for Richard. He had been a brilliant and wonderful father and he and Ronnie adored each other. Why burst the family love bubble? Why give the nomadic Antonio any reason for staying in her life? It was a secret between her and Richard, kept for all those years. Richard had been there when Antonio wasn't. It was all right for him to swan off as quickly as he'd swanned in – after charming the knickers off her, literally.

Richard had promised her security and fatherhood for her unborn child. He'd soothed her emotional scars. Steady, dependable Richard. How could she be anything other than supportive of Ronnie? Minerva's own mother had never known her plight; nobody had. Only Richard. She wondered if the secret that had brought them together had eventually been the wedge that had driven them apart.

Minerva was still thankful for small mercies like Richard. Although no longer the faithful husband, he was ever the doting father and kept up his role very well from a distance. Secrets seem to spawn distance, thought Minerva. How very interesting. She was determined it wouldn't happen now.

'What am I going to do, Mum?' Ronnie searched her mother's faraway gaze.

'Not worry, for a start,' said Minerva, darting up and out to the kitchen. 'As I said, doctor's first and we'll go from there. Now then…time for another cuppa, don't you think?'

Mother, you're amazing. Ronnie closed her eyes.

Minutes later, she opened them to the clink of glasses and a brandy bottle sitting on the coffee table. She caught the twinkle in her mother's eye, as she poured out two generous measures.

'Under the circumstances, this seemed a much better idea,' said Minerva.

* * *

Saturday night came round quickly for Ronnie, and the Old Druid beckoned. She was in a strange state of limbo, where the pendulum of life swung back and forth and she found herself neither here nor there but everywhere at once. It made her feel heady and sick and yet almost euphoric at times. She was getting used to it.

She couldn't help but feel excited. Joe would be there – with Posh Bird, no less – but he would be there with his band. She pictured his face in her bedroom window, she saw his scruffy hair and cheeky grin staring back at her, and she smiled at him. She pressed her lips to the glass and the cold, wet surface was a painful reminder of all that wasn't there, but just might be, if she could only imagine harder.

The loud knock on the door didn't wait for an answer but opened wide, to reveal her mother, wrapped in a towel and still dripping from her bath.

'Ron, have you seen my purple top?' asked Minerva. 'The one with the scooped neckline and lacy bits?'

'You mean the crushed-velvet one?' asked Ronnie, delving into a drawer.

'Yes! Have you got it?'

Ronnie shrugged. 'Not here, Mum…try the airing cupboard…where are you off to anyway?'

'I told you,' said Minerva. 'It's this Faith and Fun night at the church.'

'Oh yes… The new vicar…and his *instrument*!' Ronnie stifled a giggle.

'If you're referring to his guitar, then yes… Who knows what musical delights await us?' Minerva called from the depths of the airing cupboard. 'That's if I manage to get there…'

'Didn't Isis say he was dishy?'

'Yes, well…' said a flustered Minerva. 'I'm certainly not going for the faith factor, and since fun has never entered into any Christian gathering I've ever been to, that leaves little else to get excited about don't you think?'

'Except for one thing!' laughed Ronnie. 'You could be about to meet Adonis…the new vicar…now that would be fun! But if it all goes horribly wrong and he turns out to be pants, then you could always come down the Old Druid… Joe's band is playing…should be a good one.'

'Well, that's helpful to know, if indeed Adonis does *not* match up to expectations, thank you. But I'd like to think all efforts have not been in vain…' Minerva looked down at her necklace.

Ronnie took a closer look at the small, squashed currants around her mother's neck. 'What the hell are they?' Strung in an awkward fashion on green garden string, they were hardly attractive.

'*These*, dear daughter, are juniper berries! A *simple love spell*, according to my book – although I'm not entirely convinced of that. After an unsuccessful harvest and a fraught road trip with poor old Mr Morris breaking down on the way, I finally acquired the berries and spent an age threading the darn things on to the only string I could find. Perhaps simple is *not* the best way of describing it so far!'

She was interrupted by a loud knock at the front door.

'Oh well, may the magic be with you, Mum.' Ronnie planted a kiss on her mother's hot cheek and flew down the stairs. 'Sophia's here… See you later!'

'Enjoy yourselves, girls!' sang Minerva down the stairs, as the front door slammed behind them.

Regarding her outfit, Minerva was eager to make a good impression. Having given up the hunt for the missing top and not usually one to conform, or even care what others thought of her, she wondered if perhaps it might go in her favour to be a little less Minerva and a little more (Holy) Mary on this occasion. However, it just didn't feel right. This vicar was

73

already cramping her style, and she hadn't laid eyes on him yet. There's no denying it, she thought, as she pulled the heavy folds of crushed velvet over her head and laced up the bodice of her dress: The Witch is in me and I shall not change for any man or God… Adonis or not.

* * *

Isis let herself in to Crafty Cottage and walked like an Egyptian through the hall, led by the beat and pound of crashing drums from the living room. Anticipating the rest of the night would be somewhat less energetic, she joined Minerva on the dance floor and made a quick transformation from Egyptian to Dervish. The two dancers revved themselves up, whirled around and strutted about in true belly dancing style. It was the traditional pre-night out ritual.

Minerva passed the brandy bottle to her friend and the pair of them guzzled and whirled until they fell backwards on to the sofa, squawking with laughter.

'Can't beat a good old boogie, can you, Ice?' panted Minerva, fanning herself with the end of her huge sleeves.

'No, you certainly can't,' gasped Isis in short, heavy breaths.

'What time is this thing on?' said Minerva, inspecting her glass.

'Crikey we'd better shoot,' said Isis to her watch.

With that, they bolted for the front door and out into the night air like two fireworks.

* * *

'I have to say,' said Minerva, as they approached the church door, 'this is a strange way to be spending a Saturday night, don't you think, Ice?'

Isis had got quite used to strange things since they had become friends, and didn't see the strange in it at all. It all seemed perfectly normal. Minerva, however, did appear to be unusually nervous, in spite of the amount of brandy she'd consumed.

'We're here now, let's make the most of it,' said Isis.

Minerva grappled with her bag, pushing the brandy bottle down as far as she could and breathing in hard as she followed Isis into the church. They were directed to the room at the back by Mrs Selby, one of those very nice sorts of village people, who lived in a very nice little cottage, and only said very nice things to everybody, in a very nice way.

'Do go and help yourselves to tea and coffee,' she said nicely. 'Or a glass of wine, if you wish… No charge, but if you'd like to make a donation…' and she very nicely pushed the donation box under their noses, with the nicest of smiles.

Having done with the niceties, they filed through and hovered around the refreshments table, Minerva especially, gravitating towards the plastic cups and the wine.

'Wasn't expecting *this*,' whispered Minerva, as she reached for a cup.

'It'll save on the rocket fuel.' Isis glanced nervously at Minerva's bag.

'You're absolutely right, Ice – that'll do for a nightcap later. But, for now, this'll do nicely,' she said, winking at Isis, while pouring the wine into a plastic cup and smiling at Mrs Selby. 'Although not quite the holy grail, is it?'

Isis felt her toes curl and glanced nervously down at her open sandals. She concentrated hard on her breathing and was determined *not* to have one of those silly panic attacks. She should be used to Minerva by now. But really, in a *church* of all places.

Meanwhile, Minerva was warming up and scanning the room for a dog collar. She noticed a guitar propped up at the end of the aisle, standing to attention by the altar. It was shiny and new looking, but without any sign of its owner.

'Hello, how's it all going?' The sing-song lilting voice seemed to come from nowhere. She was a sucker for an Irishman. His hands reached out towards hers, long and slender. The handshake was firm and warm. She liked that.

Her eyes worked their way up the brushed cotton sleeve...tartan? She wasn't sure about that...blue? Not a bad colour...safe. Ah yes, the dog collar... Well, she'd been expecting it. She could get used to it, at a push.

'The name's David McAlister. I'm very pleased to meet you... What a lovely village you have here!' Two dark eyes flashed at Minerva and she smiled back instantly. He was a smooth operator.

'Thank you... Yes, *we* like it.' She stumbled a little over her words. 'I'm Minerva, and this is Isis.'

'Well, it's a pleasure to meet you both,' he said, looking at Minerva. 'I look forward to getting to know you better, through the course of the evening and...in the future.'

She couldn't take her eyes off him. His elfin face and close-shaven beard had an undoubtedly ethereal quality. *He's the spit of Errol Flynn*, thought Minerva as images of forests and trees sprang into her mind. She'd always fancied herself as Maid Marian.

'But, for now, I must make a start.' He gestured towards the guitar. 'Do make yourselves comfortable and enjoy the night.'

He turned and walked up the aisle with a hint of a swagger.

She noticed his dark, wavy hair, loosely tied in a ponytail, and wondered if he ever got it caught in his dog collar. At this point, Minerva was very nicely confused and, grabbing Isis, began a wobbly walk down the aisle towards a front-row seat.

'Not a bad piece of cloth candy, eh, Ice?' said Minerva, before losing her footing and stumbling over some unfortunate person, innocently perched at the end of a row of pews.

Isis looked on in horror, but not surprise. Her cheeks burned with embarrassment, her hairline sprouted fine beads of sweat and her feet began to slide around in their sandals.

Minerva had had a skinful. Somehow, she managed to regain what little composure she had left and continue tottering down the aisle. When she could go no further, she slumped down hard on the nearest pew and called out to the front, loudly: 'Right…we're all ears now, vicar… Go for it!'

This was not a normal, good start for a new vicar – or in fact, any vicar in the parish (especially if one is trying to create a good impression). But Minerva was far from the norm and so good behaviour could not be expected – just as you would never expect a dog not to howl at the moon.

However, it was certainly a test of David McAlister's patience and professionalism as he watched the unlikely scene unfold before him and wondered what on earth he'd let himself in for. Eventually, with a dignified smile to the audience, he held on to his crucifix, prayed to the Creator and picked up his guitar.

6

More Tea Vicar?

The Old Druid heaved with party goers. They swilled with great gusto from small bottles and danced and fired like party poppers from every darkened corner into every available space. It had to be done. The band had rocked all night long, infecting everyone with their driving energy and transporting them to another time and place. It was the sign of a good gig.

The night was drawing to a close and the Planet Reapers were on their third encore. The sweat poured off Joe as he played like a demon and sang his heart out. The crowd loved the original songs and their enthusiasm made up for all the blood he'd sweated while creating them. The band had built up quite a following locally and he had dreams of making it big like any musician does when the scent of fame lingers close enough. The dream kept him going, but it was always the crowd that carried him to the greatest heights. Coming back down to earth again was never easy.

After bumping and grinding in all directions, Ronnie and Sophia collapsed in a heap.

'Where did Posh Bird go? Haven't seen her for ages,' said Ronnie, scanning the room.

'Think I saw her leaving earlier,' yawned Sophia, 'with an older guy…her father, possibly?'

Ronnie nodded slowly. 'Perhaps I can talk to Joe before the end of the night, now she's out of the way.'

The band silently packed up their gear, savouring the last dregs of the buzzing energy still in the room. Joe hated anti-climaxes. He bounded over to see the girls as they finished off their drinks, flushed and smiling and still pumping with adrenalin.

'Well, ladies, did you have a good night?'

'Brilliant, Joe, thanks,' Sophia burst out. 'You were great!'

'The new songs are good,' said Ronnie, more quietly. 'Love the lyrics.'

'You think so?' Joe was always impressed when anyone had cared enough to listen properly. 'Thanks, Ron; you never know how a song will go down until you've gigged it, but they felt pretty good.'

She wanted to ask him where Posh Bird was, and if they were still an item, and if he could ever like herself more than just a friend. She wanted to tell him that she missed him, that she'd made a big mistake and didn't know what to do. She wanted to tell him that she was scared and in trouble. But she couldn't.

She laughed and carried on as usual. She was good at hiding her feelings and even better now at being someone she wasn't and never would be again. She wanted to tell him that she loved him. But she didn't. She looked quickly away from him – aware that her gaze was a little too intense – and over to the other side of the room.

Ernie had his work cut out behind the bar, but fortunately

had an extra pair of hands, in what looked to Ronnie like the Molly Maid woman Derek had run off with. If she had bothered to look more closely, she would have realized that Derek, estranged husband of Isis, was tucked away at the far end of the bar. He'd been hugging half a pint all night, never once taking his eyes off the Molly Maid, reeking of neediness and dependency. Isis had put up with it for years, and he'd chipped away at her until she had no self-esteem or confidence left at all. His weakness had made Derek a miserable character. Emotional bullies usually were.

There was a hustle and bustle coming from the door, and in came Minerva and Isis. *Mum's looking a bit worse for wear*, thought Ronnie, as a dishevelled Minerva weaved her way over.

'Ronnie, darling…have we missed the band? That's what happens when you go to a church social on a bloody *Saturday!* Are they still serving?'

'Only one way to find out…' Isis made her way to the bar and stopped suddenly.

She'd seen him, poised on a bar stool, looking her way. She felt sick.

'Evening, Isis, fancy seeing you here.' Derek's words sounded awkward and stilted.

'It's my local,' she said defensively.

'Bar's closed!' Molly Maid spat at the stragglers.

'Is Ernie around or is it just *you?*' Brandy-fuelled or not, Minerva could sniff out a rat anywhere.

Isis breathed a sigh of nervous relief.

Molly Maid looked quickly at Derek and then back to Minerva. 'He's out the back, bottling up.'

'Would you be so kind as to run along and *fetch* him for me, then?' Minerva narrowed her eyes and rested her elbows on the bar. Molly Maid looked at Derek – who was studying a bar mat with great intensity – and realizing the futility of her situation, strutted off in search of her boss.

Minerva sidled up to Derek and leaned heavily towards him. 'Derek! What brings you to this neck of the woods? Haven't seen you around for *ages!*'

'Yes, well, Mandy works here now, so…' Derek mumbled. 'Just here to give her a bit of…support.'

Isis coughed.

'Ah, yes, *support…*' hissed Minerva. 'Good at that, aren't you, Derek?'

'Now there's no need for that, Minerva; just here minding my own…'

'…business? Is that it, Derek? Oh, and it's none of mine… *I do beg your pardon!*'

She knew he'd never liked her, insidious little man that he was. She'd always been a threat to his power over Isis.

Ernie appeared, wide-eyed and slightly out of breath. 'Minerva, what can I get you?'

'Ah, Ernie, you're a love. The usual, two, please?' She flashed her eyes and teeth at him, well aware that his gaze had slipped down to the two assets he found far more attractive.

'Oh well, no doubt *Mandy* will enjoy her time at the Old Druid.' Minerva continued talking to Derek, ignoring the fact that Molly Maid Mandy was standing, rather nervously, in front of her. 'It's a wonderful pub, and we do love our local, don't we, Ice?'

Derek winced.

'Err…yes, we do,' said Isis, toying with her hair-piece.

'Anyway, must go and talk to my daughter and her friends. See you later!' Minerva didn't even look at him as she spun round and left him, glaring after her.

Derek was seething, Mandy was powerless, and Ernie was beaming from ear to ear.

Minerva sniggered to herself as she joined the others.

'Joe! How lovely to see you.' She threw her arms around him. 'Minerva, I see you're in fine form, as usual.'

'Well, wouldn't anyone be, after a night of Faith and Fun?'

'And where was that, may I ask?' said Joe. 'I hope it was good, you missed our gig for it.'

'The church, of all places, would you believe?' Minerva giggled. 'With the new vicar and...' she paused, 'his *instrument*, no less.'

'Tell us more, Mum.' Ronnie was intrigued.

'Well... *David* played his guitar and said the odd godly thing although he spared us the happy clappy stuff, which I have to say, I really would have objected to – and, considering it all went on in the church, it wasn't a bad debut for this new *man of the cloth*.'

Blimey, thought Ronnie, she'll be going to Bible classes next.

'So, what *did* he play on his guitar, then?' asked Joe.

'All of his own compositions, Joe,' said Isis. 'Not bad at all, actually.'

Joe looked impressed.

'Although perhaps it would've been better if the lyrics hadn't been quite so *nice*,' said Minerva, swigging back her drink.

'So tell us, Minerva,' said Sophia, 'what's he like?'

Minerva's eyes lit up. 'Well, if you can imagine an Errol Flynn- type...'

The three younger faces looked blank.

'Okay...' she pondered. 'Maybe Johnny Depp...ish.'

'What? No way!' Sophia and Ronnie sang in unison.

'Well…almost,' said Minerva. 'Give or take the un-godliness aspect, of course.'

'Only if you think Johnny Depp is *not* a god, Minerva,' said an indignant Isis.

'The point is, mother,' said Ronnie, 'whether this David is *god- like* himself?'

'He's not quite Adonis but, as Isis and myself have concluded so far, not bad for a bit of cloth candy.' She winked at Isis.

'Must you reduce the poor man to such a derogatory description?' said Isis, horrified.

'Yes, I must…' Minerva pouted, '…for two reasons. One: He's not here and two: I don't care!'

'Anyway, Mum, when's your next date with David?' teased Ronnie. 'Tomorrow morning at ten?'

Minerva shot her a wicked smile. 'Very funny, Ron. No, I shan't be making the ten o'clock Sunday service… However, I am thinking about joining the book club he's starting up in the week. Should be fairly safe ground, I think, don't you?'

'When's that on, Minerva?' Isis twitched and so did her hairpiece.

'Thursday evening, I think he said.'

'That's our belly dancing night,' Isis whispered.

'Oh well, needs must I'm afraid, Ice.'

Minerva's sweeping gesture floored Isis. To be cast aside so easily was a pattern instigated by Derek – and one she thought she'd broken, with Minerva's help… How ironic and cruel life was!

Ronnie looked away. It was too painful to watch.

Oblivious to the damage she was doing, Minerva turned to the others. 'So where's the party, you lot?' she asked, banging on the table like an auctioneer. 'I haven't finished yet.'

* * *

Over the next week, the pendulum swung between Ronnie's dilemma and the new vicar's clothly capers. When she found herself worrying over one, Minerva would turn her mind to the other, focusing on anything that entered her thoughts and stayed there long enough to lighten her mood and cheer her up. It seemed to create enough light and shade to keep her hormone-battered emotions in check, while her imagination kept her entertained with all sorts of colourful scenarios. The new vicar did appear to have potential – but would it be enough for her?

David McAlister seemed to behave like a gentleman – but, she wondered, was he too nice? Perhaps she needed someone like Antonio again, to really get her blood going? Another roaming Romeo, who would love her and leave her? No, she didn't think so. She pondered on Ronnie's predicament and remembered her own, all those years ago. She'd been so scared. The least she could do was be there for her daughter, whatever she decided to do.

Maybe she'd have more of an idea by now…after her doctor's appointment. Minerva found herself walking from room to room, like a caged animal. She grabbed her beloved tarot cards and focused on the most positive outcome for Ronnie.

The Queen of Wands popped out first, a character Minerva had always associated with herself – fiery, dynamic, confident and strong-willed. Of course, she played an important part, there was no doubt about that. The next card was the Three of Wands: expansion and direction; a good time for long-term planning and having the clarity to see ahead. The final card was the King of Pentacles: a steady, dependable male, with a good head for money. Well, that was Richard, of course. He had plenty of the stuff and knew how to make it *and* handle it. Oh yes, he had the Midas touch, did Richard.

It was quite clear to Minerva that Ronnie's fate lay sandwiched between the secure foundations of her parents' love. She'd have to tell Richard, and he'd surely come round to the idea, and provide her with all she needed financially, which was more than Minerva could afford on her own. With her parents by her side to support her, Ronnie would be able to see a way ahead and plan for the future, to bring this little person into the world. It all made perfect sense and brought great comfort to Minerva – but she couldn't resist pulling one more card, to see what would happen next...

As soon as she looked at it, she wished she hadn't asked at all. Why did she have to push those psychic boundaries? Overstepping the mark was one of her Goddess-given traits, it would seem. The Five of Wands glared out from the pack, speaking of challenges, struggles and conflict. As if, deep down, she didn't know that. As if she could assume that everything was just going to fall into place and end happily ever after. As if Ronnie would know exactly what to do, and would do it. As if the destructive force of fear was going to dissipate and transmute into love without a battle. As if.

I should know better, she thought. I should know that nothing is ever that simple. *Life* is not that simple. The cards always revealed what she already knew, but maybe didn't always realize, at least not at first. But it really wasn't that hard to see, for anyone.

When the front door opened, heralding Ronnie's return, she whispered a word of thanks to the tarot spirits and hurriedly put them away.

'How did it go, love? What did the doctor say?'

Ronnie sank down heavily. 'Well, she asked me if it was planned, if I was in a relationship, asked me what I wanted to do… Then she told me the…options… and said I needed to think carefully and take everything into account.'

'Right, I see,' said Minerva, in a hushed voice.

'I need to act fairly quickly if…' Ronnie trailed off and looked at her mother.

'…if you want to terminate the pregnancy?' Minerva said, as calmly as she could. 'Is that what you want?'

She must try and stay neutral. She must. She mustn't influence Ronnie in this at all, if she could help it. She had to make her own decision. 'Do you want to talk to your father?'

'I'm not sure that's a good idea,' said Ronnie.

'He might surprise you, Ron. Sometimes people react completely differently to how you imagine they will.'

'Yeah, but I'm not sure that he needs to know.' 'Oh, I see…' said Minerva. 'You've decided, then?'

'Look, Mum, how the hell am I going to manage with a baby? How is that going to fit into my life?'

I managed!

Minerva couldn't ignore the desperation in her daughter's voice – but she felt desperate, too, and was re-living that same moment, that same decision that she had been faced with nineteen years ago. She needed to talk to Richard. He would know what to do…

'I really think your father will…'

'No, Mum! I don't want him to… I don't want him involved.' Ronnie was adamant.

Here comes the Five of Wands, thought Minerva. The struggle had started and she didn't know if she had the energy for it, not with Ronnie. It was just too painful.

The rap of the door knocker was an unwelcome intrusion, and yet they both felt a strange sense of relief.

'Who the bloody hell is that?' Minerva got up to answer it, 'David!' She gasped.

He was as good an actor as he was a gentleman: 'Good morning to you, Minerva! I hope you don't mind, but I wondered, if you weren't busy…' He looked past her and into the hallway, '…if perhaps you wouldn't mind me boring you with the agenda for the book club? I would appreciate someone to run through it with.' He held her gaze. 'That's if you're not doing anything, of course?'

'I'm going down the yard now, Mum.' Ronnie came flying out of the front room and shot up the stairs.

'Oh… Okay, darling; yes, that sounds like a good idea.' Minerva called up the stairs.

She turned to the shining Adonis on her doorstep. 'Come in, David; it's lovely to see you… A cup of tea?'

* * *

Ronnie had never been so glad of Bob's company. She balanced on the field gate and reached across to his grubby dreadlocks and pulled them towards her. He gave no resistance, only leaning in to her as she buried her face in his neck.

'Hey, boy,' she whispered.

He knew all about her. She didn't need to tell him anything. That was the good thing about horses: they had special ways…magical ways.

That's why she loved Bob. She never had to tell him anything and, even though he knew all about her, he never told anyone.

They had secrets. They trusted each other.

She breathed heavily into the grubby neck, thick with his winter coat, and was jolted backwards as Bob pulled away sharply. Something had startled him. Kismet was trotting across the field towards them, calling out as she did so. That could only mean one thing...

Ronnie turned around to see Sophia strolling towards the gate, a couple of broken carrots in her hand. She smiled and said nothing, just passing half a carrot to Ronnie who gave it to a hungry Bob.

The girls stood in comfortable silence and watched their animals chewing and spitting orange foam as the carrots went down in muffled slurps. It was a comforting noise.

'How did it go at the doc's?' asked Sophia at last.

'Okay,' said Ronnie. 'Now I have to make the decision.'

'That sucks.'

Ronnie shrugged. 'Yeah, it all sucks, if you ask me.' She patted Bob's neck hard and started walking slowly back to the stables. Sophia followed.

'I thought you had already made your mind up, Ron.' Sophia joined Ronnie on a straw bale outside the stables.

'I had...almost...'

'What's changed?'

'It's Mum. She's been really good – a star, really. But she had this look on her face when I came back from the doctor's...when I was telling her...' She picked off a piece of straw and began to twiddle it in her fingers. 'She looked...well, hurt, I suppose.'

'She's bound to be upset, Ron.'

'You're not getting it. It was as if she wanted me to have the baby and didn't...'

'…want you to have an abortion? She said that?'

'No! She never said that. She was as cool as a cucumber about it really… Apart from the fact she thinks my Dad should be involved.'

'And what do you think about that?'

'I'd rather he wasn't. If I'm going to…get rid of it, then why does he need to know? It would just cause more of a fuss and I don't think I could honestly cope with any more input from *anyone*. I know it sounds harsh but…'

'No, it's perfectly understandable…You've got enough on your plate.'

'*Exactly,* so why would I want to add to all that by…having a baby? Wouldn't it be madness?'

Sophia shuffled around on the bale. 'Look, Ronnie, I can't answer that for you. I can only imagine what it must be like and I don't envy you…*at all.* But what I do know is that I couldn't do it, have the baby I mean. I couldn't do it on my own, not without being in a proper relationship. But then again, I don't have a mother like yours. My parents would be devastated, they're terribly old school. But your mother is totally different.' She smiled at Ronnie.

'I know she has her…quirks…but she has a good heart,' Ronnie agreed. She looked at Sophia, who nodded. 'It's definitely in the right place.'

'Yes, I know, Ron – but is that a good enough reason to go through with something that is going to change your life *completely and utterly?* Have you got any idea?'

Ronnie knew she had a point.

'I know what you're saying, but is it a good enough reason to murder another human being: just so that I can keep *my life?* What about this other life?' She looked down at her stomach.

'What about that, Sophia? What is more valuable?'

'Christ, Ronnie, I don't think you can afford to be thinking like that. Not if you're going to… I mean, it's not even born yet. It's not a life really, is it?'

Ronnie sprang up and turned on Sophia.

'How can you say that? How did we begin *our lives?*'

'What about Joe?' It hit Ronnie like a sharp arrow.

'What do you mean…Joe?'

'Well…if there was any chance of you getting together…'

'But he's with *someone else!*'

'Yes, I know – at the moment. But really, can you see it lasting? I saw the way he looked at you the other night, Ron. He's into you big time; he just doesn't know it yet! Do you want to jeopardize any chance you might have with him for the sake of…?'

'…a baby?' She thought about it. 'If Joe is the person I think he is, then maybe he wouldn't mind so much!'

'That's a big *maybe* Ron. And that's one hell of a *test* to put somebody through – and to put yourself through, if it doesn't come off!'

'Look, Sophia, this is doing my head in. I don't know if I can take Joe into account that much. I know it's crazy, but I feel responsible. I want to do the right thing. Is that wrong?' She cupped her hands over her face and Sophia got up and wrapped her arms around her friend.

'Of course it's not wrong.' She stroked the mass of rumpled, dark hair. 'None of it's wrong.'

* * *

Minerva put the kettle on for the second time. She couldn't

believe how well they were getting on. David was so easy to talk to – and, as long as the subject didn't get round to religion, she was sure they'd be fine. She had no idea how open-minded he was or how he would respond to her *witchiness*, but she wasn't prepared to chance it – not yet.

She chuckled to herself. Little did he know it, but he was already under her spell. She felt for the juniper berries around her neck and smiled. The power of magic never ceased to amaze her. What would a man of the cloth think of that, then?

'I see you have some tarot cards Minerva,' David had spotted them on the side table.

'Oh...yes,' said Minerva slowly. 'Well...they're not actually mine... They're Ronnie's, my daughter's.'

'Interesting! My grandmother used to read the tarot. She was always using them. They held quite a fascination for me as a child... They still do, in fact.'

Minerva couldn't speak. She fussed around with the cups and stirred them again with the teaspoon, while she tried to collect her thoughts. He was into the *tarot*? Was it allowed? How did that fit in with his job description?

'Can you read them?' she asked.

'I haven't for years...but yes, my grandmother taught me... She was a very gifted lady.'

This can't be happening, thought Minerva; he's got to be joking, surely. A man of the cloth, the village vicar – not only did he play the guitar *in church* – but he read the tarot.

She nearly spat her coffee out... It was beyond weird. 'Doesn't it...interfere with your...beliefs?' *Damn, I was going to steer clear of this*, she thought.

'Well, I don't see why it should, really. There are a lot of misconceptions surrounding the cards and the magical arts.

They are an ancient and spiritual tool – in the right hands, of course. People are wary and fearful of what they don't understand, and consequently paint a dark picture of anything that scares them. The tarot has had a bad press, but I prefer to see it as another tool that connects us to the divine, to God... Do you see?'

'I see what you mean...yes.' She couldn't have put it better herself. 'It's wonderful that you see them as part of a spiritual tradition that connects us all...'

'Absolutely. Have you ever thought of learning yourself, Minerva?'

'Yes, well I am...you could say *dabbling* a bit. I don't mean 'dabbling', as in... What I really mean is, I'm learning.'

Well, it wasn't lying completely. One never stopped learning did one?

'And, like you, I do find them fascinating.' She looked right into his eyes.

This man had a depth to him that she'd never come across before. It stimulated and excited her, and she felt the stirrings of something she thought was long buried. It's that sexy kundalini serpent, she thought: coiled up and sleeping for far too long.

He looked straight back at her, dark eyes glistening against pale skin, and she realized how ethereal he appeared, and not in the least out of place in her magical living room. A large oil painting of the Green Man loomed behind him, and she thought how a forest-green aura became one so heavenly. The Goddess Hecate shone her formidable brass presence from above the fireplace across the room. Hanging wooden pentacles swung with dream weavers from the beams, and crystals sparkled from the mantelpiece to the bookshelves. As candles volleyed for position everywhere, it would be hard to assume that this was anything other than a sacred space, a spiritual sanctuary. It was home to her and Ronnie, and they loved it.

Who am I trying to kid? She mused. Certainly not David McAlister, that was for sure. He was a striking specimen of contrasts, both inside and out. Dark, closely cropped hair, grown long at the back and pulled into a neat ponytail, it didn't really go with the dog collar – but neither did much else, she decided.

'Anyway, Minerva...the book club.'

She liked that commanding tone. 'Yes, where were you thinking of holding it: the room at the back of the church?' The obvious choice, she thought.

'Actually, no... As a separate thing altogether. I think it needs to be in a neutral venue somewhere else, don't you?'

She didn't know anything anymore. 'Have you...anywhere in mind?'

'Well, I thought the Old Druid looked a favourite. Central for people and convenient, don't you think?'

'Have you been there yet?' Minerva asked.

'No. I was wondering if perhaps you would join me on my first visit?' The flash of those dark eyes catching the light, reminded her rather oddly of the Devil.

'I'd be delighted,' said Minerva, rolling the juniper berries between her fingers.

7

Brandy Comes Before a Fall

Ronnie needed time to think. She found herself cycling the long way home from the stables, with thoughts and pedals going round as fast as each other. It would have been therapeutic if she hadn't felt so sick, but at least she felt like she was getting *somewhere* in her head...kind of. Dad always said that when working out a problem, you had to weigh up the pluses and the minuses, and she'd done that.

Surely, it was easy wasn't it? You went with the majority.

Forcing herself to be logical, she tried to work it out and figured she'd already used up most of her emotional resources and was heading for depletion. Maths had never been her favourite subject but it did have its uses.

The trouble was, she kept seeing babies everywhere. They were in prams, buggies, straddled on hips like koalas, perched awkwardly on shoulders. *Cocooned in bellies.* There was no escaping them. They were like an army descending upon her world to defend themselves, to fight for their rights. They were on buses and billboards. They were in streets and shops. They were on the front cover of magazines. They were on washing powder packets and milk cartons. They were on the telly. They were in doctors' waiting rooms.

They were invading her world.

She remembered her mother's fortieth birthday, some years ago. All those stupid cards with *Life Begins at 40!* What rubbish. Why wait till the middle of a life to start living? Why not start at the beginning? When *was* the beginning? *When did life begin?*

She felt she was only just beginning to know, to understand some of it. It was her life and it was happening to her. This was *her experience*. She felt her mind getting bigger...opening up and expanding.

On she pedalled, down the narrow lane, deep in thought, when the squawk of a pheasant behind the hedge startled her. The bike wobbled and she stamped a foot to the ground to steady it and looked across to the field beyond.

There he was again.

An imposing sight in his long cloak, wizened face half shrouded by its baggy hood, the Hermit turned and grinned at Ronnie and she felt a wave of calm come over her as she smiled back.

'Ah yes, so many questions, young lady.' The velvet tones came from the earth itself. 'I am pleased to make your acquaintance once again and I notice you are pondering upon life's many mysteries...and this is a good thing. For only when we reach out and search, do we find ourselves closer to what we are looking for.' The Hermit looked across the field to the horizon.

'I'm not entirely sure what that is...at the moment,' said Ronnie, following his gaze. 'All I know is how confused I am. Nothing makes much sense.' She felt a tightening in her throat and gripped hard at the handlebars.

'Trying to make sense of something which is not in harmony with who you truly are will only cause further conflict,' said the old man. 'The soul is supreme in its ability to navigate the path to your true purpose, but you must give it the opportunity to do so. Reflect on what is the truth for you, as you see it and as you understand it. I cannot tell you what that is, for it's a quest that is your own – and only by seeking in your own way will it eventually provide the answers that you look for. I can, however, say this – for, troubled as you are, there is clarity within your reach.' He leaned on his staff towards her. 'Remove the obstacles of doubt and uncertainty, for they will remain in your way as long as you give them attention. Recognize that change is inevitable and signifies all that has been outgrown. Let go of what no longer serves you and embrace the unknown, for it gravitates towards you, whether you like it or not.'

The sound of laughter rang through the damp air and Ronnie stared wide-eyed at the Hermit. This peculiar old man from the magical realms was sharing his timeless wisdom with her. Why? What was so special about her? Did she deserve it…after what she'd done?

'And why not, indeed?' His words sang out, and the brightest blue eyes pierced her soul. 'What makes you so unworthy? Yes, you are young and yes, there is much to learn…of course there is! Mistakes are your lessons: how else will you learn? But we are given signs all the time. And if we are wise enough to trust in the instinct of the inner voice, it will teach us and show us the way. It will lead us to act. And what we thought we'd find outside of ourselves, we discover on the inside…always. An interesting paradox, don't you think?' He laughed again, and Ronnie frowned at him.

'But that's the problem!' She banged the front wheel of the

bike down hard. 'I don't know what to do.'

'You know more than you think, young warrior soul. Do not hide from the truth. Face it and it will guide you forwards. Trust in it. Take one step at a time.'

Ronnie was unsure how long she'd been standing by the hedge, but the car rumbling past woke her up from what seemed like a hazy dream. She blinked hard and flexed her fingers, looking over to where the Hermit had stood. She breathed in the cold, damp air and, pulling her collar tight around her neck, climbed back on the bike. Try as she might to ignore what had just occurred, the warm feeling inside would not go. She felt it spread like a stain in her chest, and she placed one cold hand on her heart, just to make sure it was real. *Follow the path of least resistance...one step at a time.* Is that what he'd meant by the inner voice?

Maybe hearts really did talk.

She knew where she had to go. The marina loomed up in front of her and she turned down the long drive and looked out for Joe.

She was pretty sure it was his lunch hour so, making her way to the tea-hut, she carried on riding at speed, to keep the momentum going, so as not to give her a reason for turning back. She wanted things to be the same between them again...as friends who could say anything to each other. As friends who laughed and cried at the same things and trusted each other. She'd missed their friendship.

'Hey, Ron!' sang a voice from above.

She looked up to see Joe, perched half-way up a boat mast, like a pirate.

'Have you had lunch yet?' She smiled up at him. 'Thought I'd join you for a change.'

'Great… I'll be with you in a sec!' He beamed down at her, and she felt the warm stain spreading in her chest again.

'Be careful!' She knew masts could be dangerous, and even more so when a boat was out of the water, on the hard standing. Bones broke easily from heights and hard landings.

It hadn't been so long ago when Ropey, one of the older boat hands, broke his pelvis in two places falling from a mast. After being air-lifted to hospital, he'd been in traction for six weeks afterwards and was still off work now, after three months. You needed your wits about you when it came to boats and water.

'Can't take anything for granted with the elements and bloody heights!' Ropey had joked from his awkward horizontal position in the ward where Ronnie and Joe had been frequent visitors. With great delight, he told them tales of embarrassing bedpan scenarios in a world that had become very small for him. The nurses, however, were the glowing highlights of his stay. He called them 'angels' and his 'guilty pleasure' – which apart, from being an absurd contradiction, had Joe and Ronnie laughing from the minute they arrived till the minute they left. You couldn't beat Ropey for entertainment value. In hospital, he turned what could easily have been a depressing situation into one of great hilarity. His buoyant spirit had saved him, he cheered everyone up and Ronnie wished she knew more people like him.

'Wanna cuppa, Ron?' Joe was on terra firma once again and she breathed a sigh of relief.

'Love one, shipmate!' She followed his brisk pace to the small, demountable building parked at the top of the slipway.

They sat among the general disarray of wet overalls, dirty boots and towering piles of boating and fishing magazines littered about the place. She always felt at home there; maybe it was because of the menfolk. She preferred their company to women: they were far easier to get along with. Men, in general were less complicated, less likely to hold grudges and far more able to laugh things off. She liked that.

'Great gig on Saturday, wasn't it?' She took the chipped mug from Joe.

Joe's eyes lit up. 'Do you know what, Ron, it's great when the crowd are behind you – and they were certainly up for it. Looked like you and your friend were enjoying yourselves.'

'Sophia? Oh, we didn't stop all night. You certainly rocked the place good and proper. Great to see you back on form, Joe!'

'Yeah, about time, eh, Ron?' He looked at her and smiled.

I wish you wouldn't do that.

'Well, everything takes time Joe – you can't rush these things.' An awkward silence fell over the room and Ronnie could've sworn Eve had just walked in. Joe's mother had a presence that even death couldn't deny her.

'No...' Joe faltered. 'Anyway, I'm glad you came to the gig, Ron; it was good to see you there.'

'What happened to *Penelope*? Did she go home early?'

He reached for a squashed pouch of Golden Virginia and delved into it, pulling out a tuft of tobacco, and began to roll up.. 'Not getting on too good at the moment,' he sighed. 'We're kind of different, the cracks are starting to show and I'm not sure where the relationship's going, to be honest.'

'Where do you want it to go?' She knew he wouldn't mind her probing.

The smoke billowed around him while he pondered. 'I'm not really sure, Ron. We got on all right at first, but I suppose it wasn't long after Mum died and I wasn't up to much. Just used to see her when she was down for the weekend with her Dad, on the boat and that. It was all about what *she* was doing and I was happy to go along with that at the time, took the pressure off me when I needed it. I didn't have to think too much about anything, really...'

'So what's changed, then?' She pushed further, knowing the answer, but she wanted to hear him say it. Verbalizing feelings gave them extra power and she knew it.

'Well, *time* changes things, don't you think? People change and I'm in a different place now than I was a few months ago... I've got better and she's got worse.'

'Joe... That's a bit cruel.'

'Oh for God's sake, Ron! Look, I'm done with sitting around feeling sorry for myself and I'm done with other people feeling sorry for me. Okay, maybe I needed that at first, but I don't need it now. I don't *want* it now, so maybe Penny doesn't fit in with what I want any more. Time to move on. Does that make sense? That's not being cruel, is it?'

'No it isn't and yes, it does make perfect sense. But are you going to let it go on or what? She really likes you, doesn't she?'

'Well, I thought she did, but I'm not so sure now...' He narrowed his eyes at her. 'Can I ask a question?'

She liked it when he asked her opinion. 'Go on, then...'

'Well, if you really liked someone, wouldn't you be pleased that they were enjoying themselves?'

'What do you mean? Are you talking about Saturday? Did she get funny about anything...jealous, maybe?'

'You could say that. Don't know what it was but anyway I'm not busting a gut to work it out. I can't be bothered, to be honest with you, Ron. I've got better things to be doing than pandering to the selfish whims of a...'

'... Posh Bird?' There, she'd said it. Clapping one hand over her mouth, Ronnie stared at Joe in mock horror.

'Ooh! Put those claws back in, Rhiannon.' He shot her a wicked grin. 'It doesn't become you!'

Ronnie giggled, leaned across and thumped him…hard.

* * *

'So, how long have you been a Witch, Minerva?'

The words rolled out of David's mouth and echoed around the bottom of Minerva's glass as she over-calculated the final swig of her drink. The last drops of brandy shot out and down her cleavage; the rest just dribbled down her chin…slowly.

Was this man for real? Not only had he recognized her witchy origins, but he was now reducing her to a complete dribbling idiot in the process. How was a woman to redeem herself at the mercy of such shrewd observations? Here was a truly cunning man – and of the cloth, too… Was there no end to his talents?

'Can I just ask how you know?'

He's going to tell me I remind him of his grandmother.

He had the audacity to chuckle, which did nothing to pacify Minerva – in fact, it downright irritated her.

'I'm sorry, forgive me. But without putting it too plainly…'

'You can put it as plainly as you like,' she said frostily, 'I won't be offended.'

'Minerva, please…' he raised both hands. 'You have pentacles adorning your cottage…and, indeed, yourself.' He nodded at her large, silver, pentacle ring and the pentacle tattoo on the inside of her left wrist, '…as well as various other give-aways, from the Green Man to the tarot, to the way you just *are*. It is not a judgment, I assure you, only an observation, and…' his look softened, 'I approve whole-heartedly…really I do.'

Oh! Do you now?

He waited until he'd finished before lowering his hands.

That's a sign of repentance, if ever I saw one, thought Minerva and cleared her throat. 'I would like to inform you, David, that I do not need, nor do I *seek* anyone's approval. I am my own person and *completely* at ease with who I am. And, as we are on the subject of labels, if we *must* define ourselves in such a way, then…WITCH…' She paused for what seemed an age, '…is what I am very happy to be called and known as. To answer your first question: to the best of my knowledge, I have been a Witch all of this life and, as far as I'm aware, most of my previous lives, too. That is, apart from the one before last, when I was a Roman orgy planner, who – although having no connection to the Craft itself - had everything to do with my idea of how to throw a wild party and have a good time, and still does. *Plus* it's also where I got my name, according to my mother, who was regressed while pregnant with me.'

Wrap that round your guitar and stuff it up your dog collar, she thought.

'Would you care for another drink, Minerva?' David asked, getting to his feet.

'Thank you. A large brandy, minus the hemlock juice, will do nicely.'

The drink seemed to appear almost immediately and, concentrating hard, Minerva sipped it with the utmost decorum, while David chatted to Ernie and made a few vicarly introductions to some locals sitting at the bar. It was all very surreal and yet bizarrely stimulating. This was not the normal turn of events by any stretch of the imagination, and she wondered if it had anything to do with her hormones. Could it be that, in their unbalanced state, they were attracting people and situations of a similar disposition – and therefore she could not be held at all responsible? Perhaps it was an act of the hormone Gods? If that was the case, she couldn't possibly take him seriously. Perhaps he wasn't really a vicar and had blagged his way into the parish and the vicarage and was about to blag his way into her. Would she mind? Of that she wasn't sure – and, as the brandies slipped down, she found herself minding even less.

'So where were we?' asked David, returning to his seat. 'Ah yes, the subject of your witchiness…intriguing, I'm sure.'

Oh really?

'Yes, well, can we change the subject, do you think? I'm not about to give you my life story. No doubt it'll come out sooner or later, but for now…what about *you* Father David?'

'What do you want to know, oh lady of magic and mystery?'

'Well…why a man like you is wearing *that*?' She pointed a finger at his dog collar.

'Because I'm a man of God, of course.'

'And who *is* your God?' she demanded.

'He's a good bloke, Minerva, worth getting to know.' He winked and picked up her hand, which was sweating profusely. 'A bit like myself…'

She could feel him getting under her skin. It was another one of those good – with a great deal of potential to be bad – moments. The rebel in her cried out as the heat began to course through her veins. She felt the wet hair at the back of her neck and knew she was heading for an eruption of some kind, but wasn't sure what.

She stared at the hazy form in front of her. 'What are your views on spontaneous combustion?'

He kept hold of her hand and leaned forward to look down at her well worn and much loved Dr Martens. 'I don't see any signs of it at the moment.'

'Are you sure?' She kept her eyes on him, not daring to look down.

'I'm certain,' he said. 'Your boots, Minerva, are well and truly occupied. The moment that changes, I will let you know...' He thought for a second. 'Are you okay? You do look a little warm.'

She had definitely changed colour. Even her shoulders and neck were red. At least I'll be glowing with all this heat, she thought, and that's not a bad thing.

'Do I look it?' She flapped the loose neckline of her top, to let out some air.

'Do you want some water?' David headed for the bar.

She placed her hands around her neck and felt a warm stickiness. *She* may not have combusted, but the juniper berries had. She gasped at the blue stains on her fingers and rummaged in her bag for a tissue.

Was the spell working or not? Could it be *un-working?* Whatever it was doing, she was pretty sure a hot-flushed neck covered in blue stains was not the most appealing of sights on any level. Blue and red made purple and that spelt horror.

Things were going from bad to worse.

'Drink this.' He handed her some water in a pint glass.

'Thanks.'

It was cold and hit the back of her throat like an iceberg. After much coughing and spluttering, she eventually managed to compose herself. 'I think I need to get some fresh air.'

'Of course; shall we go?' She didn't think him presumptuous at all. In fact, she quite liked the thought of being looked after, and didn't care at all for the idea of spontaneously combusting on her own. At least if it happened with David, he could give her boots to Ronnie, who would bury them in the garden. Being committed to the earth was definitely more attractive than going up in smoke. Better to be grounded. She'd rather be a pile of dirt than a pile of ashes.

'Lean on me, Minerva.' He sounded serious.

She was glad to get outside and found the cold air had an instant cooling effect on her. However, hot flushing aside, her balance wasn't up to much, and she leaned heavily on this man, who for some reason, in spite of who and what *he* was, accepted her for who and what *she* was. She respected him for that.

'Thanks...you really are a heavenly man.'

Not usually one to laugh at her own jokes, Minerva couldn't help herself...at all, in fact. So much so that, the more she laughed, the less control she had over any of her bodily functions. Her bladder happened to be one of them and, consequently, she was unprepared when the warm liquid dribbled down the inside of her leg.

Never had she been so thankful for the hundred-and-twenty deniers that she had pulled on with great effort earlier. Thick tights are just the thing for pissing yourself in. She would remember that.

She had thought that her long skirt would cover up the evidence, but it was more serious than she realized, especially when her legs buckled beneath her and she collapsed against a lamp post. Now, this wouldn't have been so bad had it not been so dark, but it was, and there were no street lights in the village. Except this one...outside the church.

This was her finale, it seemed. The spotlight beamed down from the heavens themselves as she leaned awkwardly against the lamp post. She would never look at a dog and a lamp post in the same light again, and had never wished for anything to be over as much as in that moment.

'Minerva…are you okay?' David's voice came from afar. 'Let me help you.'

Her reflexes, although somewhat delayed, did at least make a valiant attempt to respond to the vague message of her brain. *Do you really want him to see that you've peed yourself?*

She had seen a foal being born once at the stables with Ronnie, and they had looked on helplessly while the poor creature had tried to get up. Right now, she was that foal, legs askew and floundering. She began to snigger…first a dog and now a horse. She was behaving like an animal and she shocked herself into action by hanging on for dear life to the lamp post and making a sheer, determined effort to rise from the gutter. It was not easy but she managed it…just.

Determination usually managed to steer Minerva through most of life's challenges, especially when most other things didn't – like balance and continence. And here it came, charging to the rescue, picking her up and pushing her on, in spite of whatever was trying to stop her. Pissed she may have been, but she was not beaten.

'You're as tough as your boots, Minerva…if you don't mind me saying,' said David, before looking away and staring hard at the church.

'No, I don't mind you saying, David. I *would,* however, have minded if you'd said *old*…'

He looked puzzled.

'I mean I would've minded if you'd said 'tough as *old boots*'…' She tried to pull the thick-cotton skirt, heavy with piss, away from her legs.

'I see…' said David, frowning slightly. 'Well, I'm glad I didn't, for both of our sake.'

She'd never seen anyone look so intensely at a church before.

He coughed abruptly. 'Are you suitably recovered?'

'Yes, I'm very suitably recovered, thank you.'

She was using every bit of strength and decorum to talk and walk with some dignity. He offered her his arm. 'Shall we continue?' She took it with as much grace as anyone could muster in such an undignified situation.

All was not lost.

The next thing she remembered was waking up in a strange living room. She had no idea where she was, until she saw a pair of dark eyes peering at her from over the rim of a mug.

'Are you okay, Minerva? Would you like some coffee?' The words wafted across the room and landed with the strong aroma of coffee right under her nose.

'Where am I?' she asked, trying to make who was talking.

'You're at the vicarage,' said the faraway voice. 'We came here first as it was closer and you wanted the toilet...again.'

She sighed at the explanation, which failed to remind her of what had happened – she couldn't remember... But the coffee smelt good and she was almost sure and glad it was David.

'Is it fully loaded?' she asked.

'Yes, it's real coffee.' He reached for another mug and poured dark liquid from a tall glass jug. 'Arabica... South American...a fine balance of praline flavouring.'

'Sounds very nice...thank you,' was all she could manage to say as she took the hot mug and held it against her stomach. It felt good. 'What's the time?' She yawned.

He pointed to a corner of the large room, where a grandfather clock stood. Minerva admired the rather ornate-looking specimen and eventually found her way to the face.

'Good lord and lady...one thirty! How did it get there?'

He laughed. 'With the greatest of ease and a lot of tick tocking.'

Minerva responded with a weak smile. She loved his laugh, but hadn't heard a word of what he'd said.

'Mmm… This coffee's good,' she said. 'I'd better be off soon.'

Sliding further down into the armchair, Minerva found it hard to move.

David picked up his guitar and began to pick softly at the strings. The time for talking had passed and a musical interlude was just the right thing. Nobody had to say or do anything other than drift off into their own secret world of early morning daydreams.

Apart from the cold, damp tights still clinging to her legs, which Minerva chose to ignore, a warm and fuzzy feeling was the last thing she remembered.

8

The Green Lord and the Tower

'So you're going to keep it, then?'

'Yes, Sophia, I am.'

It was like a huge weight had slipped off her shoulders and Ronnie felt an overwhelming relief. Decisions could be very empowering.

Sophia carefully wiped the cloth along the leather straps of Kismet's bridle and thought for a moment. 'Well, if you're sure...'

'As sure as I've been about anything,' said Ronnie. 'It's not been an easy decision – you know that. But the truth is, I have to go with my feelings. It didn't feel right to...you know...the alternative... It's not for me, I'm afraid. I can't really explain it better than that.'

'You don't have to, Ron...as long as *you're* happy with what you've decided, that's the important thing. Have you told your mother?'

'I'm going to tell her later. I think she'll be pleased – although she's a bit *distracted* at the moment...' Ronnie chuckled as she lifted her saddle down from the rack and on to the wooden horse in the middle of the tack room. It was a cosy little space, with the heater blowing warm air against the early winter chill.

'And what, I wonder, would be distracting your mother from her other distractions?'

Both of them laughed. Only Minerva could prompt such a remark.

'It's this man of the cloth... *David*. She seems quite into him. I know...strange but true. She came home from the vicarage at *six o'clock* the other morning.' Ronnie raised an eyebrow at her friend. 'Said she'd fallen asleep...'

'Are you serious? Anything else?' Sophia couldn't help herself: the sweet smell of drama was music to a budding lawyer's ears at times.

'Not really – you know Mum. Not just a dark horse, but one of many colours. At the moment she's like a wild brumby...tail in the air and snorting every five minutes.'

'How funny,' said Sophia, 'especially with her being a Witch, of all things! Makes you wonder how that's all going to work, doesn't it?' She looked up at Ronnie, scrubbing away at her stirrups with hot, steamy water.

'It's beyond me. Maybe, at the end of the day, if two people are meant to be together, then nothing will stop them.' Joe's face stared up at her from the water. 'Just because their beliefs are different doesn't mean they shouldn't try, does it? I suppose it depends how open-minded they are. Mum has always been very open and doesn't oppose other spiritual beliefs, but, if she *did* have any reservations, then they would be about the church...something to do with all the people who were persecuted in the past for being different.'

'Yes, I kind of guessed that was behind her thinking – and you can't blame her in a way. She's taking a chance with *David*, then?'

'Yeah… I think she's inviting him round for dinner. Should be interesting.'

'I should say,' mused Sophia, 'especially if he's seen creeping back to the vicarage in the early hours.'

'Now *that* would be nothing short of scandalous,' said Ronnie.

* * *

Gavin could hear laughter coming from the tack room. Good; it meant that Ronnie wasn't alone, and he could tell her his news and go, without things getting too embarrassing. He was polite enough to knock before going in, and stood awkwardly at the door until the giggling stopped.

'Hi there, you two… Sounds fun in here!'

'Oh… Hi, Gavin.' The words stuck in Ronnie's throat.

Gavin dug his hands deep into his pockets. 'Just thought I'd pop in and say my goodbyes…' He scuffed his boot hard against the floor. 'I'm off next week…abroad… Got a job with my uncle,' he finished quickly.

'Oh…where are you going?' Ronnie asked.

'Australia.'

'You're going to Oz? Now *that* is cool,' said Sophia. 'It's definitely somewhere I want to go when I've finished uni!'

Ronnie suddenly felt like the odd one out. 'How come so soon?'

'Well, I've been thinking about it for a while now, and my uncle's got his own farrier business out there. He can put me through the same apprenticeship I'm doing here, but with more opportunities. And the weather's better!'

'You lucky bugger,' said Sophia. 'Christmas on the beach,

then?'

Gavin laughed. 'That's right, yeah... Anyway, got a lot to do before then. I'm going to see my brother in Scotland before I go, so today's my last one at work.' He looked sideways at Ronnie.

'Well, have a brilliant time, Gavin – I'm sure you will.' She hurried across the room and pecked him politely on the cheek like a stranger.

Sophia followed suit. 'Best of luck, Gavin! How long are you going for?'

'Not sure yet, but I do have a permit, so as long as I've got work I should be okay. It's a big country and I'd like to see it all, so...who knows? Maybe I'll see you girls in a few years, eh?' He opened the door and raised his arm without turning round.

'See you, Gavin!' They echoed behind him and fell into a hushed silence.

'Well, you'd better get a move on,' said Sophia, returning to her bucket and bridle.

'With what?'

'With telling Gavin.'

'Oh I see...' said Ronnie. 'He *was* the next one on my list. But now I'm not sure.'

Sophia threw her sponge down. 'What do you mean you're *not sure*? For God's sake Ron... It's obvious, isn't it? You have to tell him before he goes.'

'But he's buggering off to the other side of the world.'

'That doesn't make it all right to keep him in the dark.'

They glared at each other and finished their tack-cleaning in silence. Ronnie was tired of feeling guilty. She'd never had to think about so many people before. Well, she'd have to get used to it. She now had a responsibility to someone other than herself and Bob. Someone who was totally reliant on her, whose life depended on her. She'd made a decision to support that life – to *give* it a life. There was nothing else but to accept it and get on with the whole damn business.

Sophia touched her arm. 'Sorry if I upset you, Ron.'

'It's not your fault, Sophia. If I hadn't of been so bloody stupid, I wouldn't be in this mess and everything would be okay.' She sighed. 'But it's not.'

'Hey, enough of that talk. You've made your decision, haven't you? And you're right, Gavin is going, so that's another one decided for you. He's out of the picture now and it's not worth beating yourself up over… So save your energy, calm down and concentrate on looking after yourself.' She nodded to Ronnie's stomach. 'Babies grow better in a calm environment.'

'Thanks,' said Ronnie, 'I bow to your infinite wisdom.'

'Actually, I read it somewhere!'

'Who cares? It's what I needed to hear.'

'Talking of which,' Sophia tilted her head to the sound of banging hooves on stable doors, 'Somebody's trying to tell us something.'

'We'd better get those nags fed, then,' said Ronnie.

* * *

Mistletoe was such an awkward thing to hang up. Minerva loved the magic of Yuletide and the excuse to drape greenery everywhere, but where was she going to put it? The fact that she'd got some was significant in itself, and she was grateful for it. This indication of improvement in a certain area of her life filled her with delight and dread all at the same time – for it seemed an age since she'd had a good enough reason to acquire some of this potent and magical plant, so revered by the Druids.

Could she do it justice? Would she remember how to *be* with a man? And not just any man...but David, of all things bright and beautiful?

Was she, a creature of the darkest and greatest mysteries, worthy of one so holy?

So far, *not* so good, she reminded herself. The memory of a brandy-fuelled evening at the Old Druid, ending in near ruin at the vicarage in the small hours, left her cold. What was she thinking? The fact that she couldn't remember seemed a large part of the problem. Brandy had that effect on her. But then, if she hadn't felt so nervous about a date with the vicar, it wouldn't have been so bad.

No, *he'd* had that effect on her. Yes, clearly it was David's fault, she concluded, resting her eyes on the Green Lord of Yule, a masterpiece of Celtic woodwork, as he grinned down on her in the hallway.

Waving the mistletoe, she addressed her favourite wall-hanging: 'Now then, my Lord of the Green, where to hang these love berries? I really think you have enough leaves of your own,' she said. 'In fact, you're overflowing with the things. Adorned with holly and ivy you may be, and as for those antlers, they come a close second...but nothing can beat the most obvious place...' She teetered on tiptoe while carefully placing the mistletoe upon the magnificent horn protruding out of the Green Lord's hands. 'Indeed,' she began, 'what a fine specimen, my Lord! May your horn of plenty fill this place with more of the same...that's in the love department, of course. A little assistance from your good self would be most appreciated.'

Chuckling to herself, Minerva stood back and admired her

handiwork, her eyes gleaming wickedly, her mind playing imaginary scenarios and her hands tingling with excitement. She couldn't wait to get them on David and pin him under the Green Lord's horn of plenty.

This, she reminded herself, was why she loved to walk the well worn and untamed Pagan path of her ancestors. It appealed to the wild side of her nature, giving her liberty to be herself, without restriction or shame. It fuelled her with a passion that was both ancient and yet timeless: the spark of life, the spirit of magic.

Oh to marvel and meddle in the simple pleasures of human nature!

All that earthiness and fertility of the land wrapped up in the Lord of the Green...or was it David? Did it really matter? She didn't think so. What mattered were only the feelings she had at this moment, pulsing their way through her in hot waves, rising and plunging into the deepest nooks and crannies of herself she'd forgotten she had.

Palpitations are not much fun at the best of times, and combined with an oncoming hot flush, even less so. But, as Minerva's timing would have it (good or bad is only a matter of opinion), she appeared to be having both beneath the Green Lord of Yule and his horn, just as the doorbell went. After a long period of deep breathing and reassuring herself she was fine when she wasn't, she answered it. It was difficult to tell who was the more surprised: David, for having assumed Minerva wouldn't be there, or Minerva, for having assumed it wouldn't be David.

Either way, it was a pleasant one for both of them.

'Minerva,' David spluttered, 'I was just on my way back from evensong and thought I'd...'

'Pop in and see me?' Minerva managed to beam him one of her brightest smiles, in spite of the flush and palpitations. She held the door back to let him in, making sure she stood directly under the Green Lord, his horn and the mistletoe. Nobody else could have timed it more perfectly.

'You've been decorating, then?' David glanced nervously up and seemed to dither for a moment. Thankfully, the dithering passed and he composed himself as much as he could, in spite of the rather tantalizing sight of Minerva's chest heaving before him. He could see she was sweating profusely, too, poor woman. She was clearly nervous – and so he did what any decent chap would do, under the circumstances and the Green Lord: he put his arm around her.

Minerva needed no more encouragement. Swooning like a schoolgirl, she looked up at the Green Lord before turning to David, her face glistening with sweat. 'It's the Green Lord of Yule, come to bestow his blessings on us!'

'Well then,' said David, 'how can we refuse such a magical gift?'

He says all the right things, thought Minerva.

Kissing can be a messy business, and the merging of bodily fluids unavoidable in most cases, so how fortunate then for Minerva – as the sweat trickled its way around them – that David was not put off by such a minor issue, or was perhaps too much of a gentleman to say.

Things were hotting up and Minerva was melting down.

And finally, giving way to the flames of passion, she silently thanked the Green Lord and his horn of plenty for such generosity.

It was definitely something she could get used to.

* * *

Ronnie felt the soft mound of her stomach. It was getting bigger and the day had come for her second scan. Twenty-one weeks and rising. Time had flown past and she didn't know how much longer she could keep it from Joe. She was in two minds. One kept saying: *Don't tell him, don't burst the bubble!* (Since Posh Bird had flown the nest, they had resumed their old friendship and she didn't want to jeopardize that.) The other cried out: *Tell him. You've always been honest with this guy, what's the big deal?* She wanted to tell him this secret. Secrets and friendship were a bad combination, of that she was sure.

But she knew it couldn't go on for much longer. Her mother and Sophia were the only people who knew, and were sworn to secrecy. It wasn't as if it was noticeable, baggy jumpers and stretchy jodhpurs were the ideal comfy substitute for jeans, without causing too much suspicion. Nothing new there, she lived in them all the time anyway.

'Ronnie, come on, love... We don't want to be late!'

She'd forgotten they were going in good old Mr. Morris. It would take at least twice as long to get there – and no, she didn't want to be late. She pulled on a baggy top over her leggings and joined Minerva on the drive.

'I really must get this door fixed.' Minerva huffed and puffed, scrambling over the passenger seat to get to the driver's side.

'Mum, you say that every time and you never do,' sighed Ronnie.

'And you reply in exactly the same way every time,' said Minerva. 'We're both clearly hanging on to an old habit. Pity, really: it's almost traditional, don't you think?'

Ronnie didn't reply. She waited patiently for Minerva to sort out her ridiculously long dress and install herself, before she climbed in beside her and waited.

The car's refusal to start was also traditional, as was Minerva's chanting of the *Magical Mr. Morris spell:* Hail Mr. Morris! You must start... bless your engine, bless your heart!

This went on for a couple of strained minutes (to Ronnie it seemed like hours), after which the constant coughing and spluttering of a tired engine laboured into action. Eventually the old car finally chugged forwards, with Ronnie discreetly checking for any spectators. One day, she thought, we'll have a car that's normal.

'Well, this is exciting, darling, isn't it?' Minerva cooed as Mr. Morris kangaroo-hopped out of the close.

Ronnie was surprised at how well her mother was taking all this. Minerva had been absolutely brilliant in turning things around and Ronnie was pretty sure she was looking forward to the arrival of the 'little person' far more than she was.

'Yeah, I suppose so,' said Ronnie, peering out the window as they drove past the marina.

'Have you told Joe yet?'

'No.'

'Don't you think he's going to notice soon, along with everyone else? It's not the sort of thing you can keep a secret forever, Ronnie.' Plus, Minerva was itching to say something to David. It already felt like she was betraying him.

'I do know that!'

'Of course you do. I was only bringing it to your attention.'

'I know, I *know*, Mum.' Ronnie sighed. 'I really want to tell him – after all, he's my best friend – but every time I go to say something...the words get stuck somehow.'

'I know what you mean, love; it's happened to me enough

times. But what is it you're worried about? What's stopping you?'

'What will he think of me? How will he feel when I tell him about something like this?' She glanced down at her stomach, and then at her mother.

'Why does it matter so much to you what he thinks and what he feels? I'm not being mean, darling; it's just that you are now deep into the realms of a situation that you can only surrender to. Let go of trying to control it. Joe is your friend; I'm sure he'll be fine about it all.'

Ronnie stared ahead at the wooden dashboard in silence.

'Oh, *I see*,' said Minerva. 'Things have changed now, have they?'

'Mum, it's not easy...'

'Nothing worth having ever is, my love. But sometimes you just have to trust that everything will turn out for the best...and it will.'

Minerva seemed so certain and Ronnie needed every bit of comforting reassurance. For all her irksome traits, her mother had a way of making her feel that everything would be all right. She so wanted to believe her.

'I hope you're right, Mum, I really do.'

'Of course I'm right, darling. When have you ever had cause to think otherwise?'

Before she could reply, Minerva stopped her and pointed to the sky. The sun pierced through the clouds like laser beams and spun out in a gold fan on to the fields. It looked like a piece of heaven.

'Trust in the magic, Rhiannon,' said Minerva with the utmost conviction, 'and it won't let you down, I'm telling you.'

* * *

'Just over six months,' said Minerva, looking up at Isis. 'She hasn't wanted anyone to know up until now.'

'Oh, I see,' said a baffled Isis. 'Who's the... I mean... I take it she's staying here...with you?'

'Yes, of course she's staying here; the father's done a runner.'

Not quite the truth, thought Minerva, but a hell of a lot easier than the rather long winded explanation she would need to give otherwise. And somehow, it didn't seem that relevant any more.

'Done a runner? Where to?'

'Oh... He's buggered off abroad somewhere, I think. Look, it's not important really...'

'*Not important?*' Isis tugged fiercely at her hair-piece. 'How can you say that, Minerva? Your daughter is six months pregnant and the cad who did it has done a runner, leaving her – if you'll pardon the expression – *holding the baby.* I don't know about you, but that sounds pretty important to me!'

Isis could be stubborn and quite fearsome at times. Minerva could see, given her present vulnerable state and in particular her attitude towards men at the moment, this probably wasn't a good time for discussing Ronnie and her news. It just showed how wrong one could be. *Note to self,* thought Minerva, *next time I decide to disclose family secrets to a friend, make sure she is in a fit enough state to receive it and not still reeling from the blows of a miserably failed marriage.* It was a recipe for disaster...poor Isis. She had suffered enough but really, this victim mentality was doing her no good.

'Isis,' said Minerva firmly, 'I can see what you're saying and yes, of course it's not *unimportant,* but it's happened and that is that, I'm afraid. What *is* important is that Ronnie has a home here, where she is loved, and the baby will have the same – with or without a father in the picture. We will manage as we all have to when life strikes a blow in our direction and knocks us off balance.' Her tone softened. 'When that happens, we have to pick ourselves up, dust ourselves down and keep going. *How* we keep going is then a choice that we have to make. We can be bitter and hold grudges and be miserable in the process, or we can decide to be good to ourselves and make room for a bit of happiness and make the best of it. What would you rather do?'

Isis stared into the distance…it was all too familiar.

She sighed and looked up at her friend. 'You're right, Minerva. I am in the process of dusting myself down at the moment and am finding the going a bit sticky, but I'll get through it, I'm sure.' She moved on briskly: 'As for Ronnie… I hadn't even noticed she looked any different. She's kept it well hidden!'

'Yes, but not for much longer,' said Minerva. 'I think she was planning to spill the beans to Joe today, when she gets back from the stables. She's quite nervous about it as they're good friends, aren't they?'

'Does she want it to be more, then?'

'I think she does, Ice. But I've said to her if it's meant to be, it will be. She doesn't really have a choice, does she? He's going to know sooner or later.'

'Do you think he feels the same for Ronnie?'

'It's one of those situations where I can't see the wood for the trees, really. I've known Joe for years and the pair of them are like brother and sister; they've grown up together. So it's difficult for me to see them in any other way.'

'I know what you mean. Oh yes, good thinking...' said Isis, as she watched Minerva reach for the tarot cards. 'Let's see what they say.'

As Minerva shuffled the cards, something niggled at her, but she didn't know what. She dismissed it and carried on the job of slotting the cards in among one other as she focused her mind on Ronnie and Joe. A card fell from the pack as she shuffled, jumping out of her hands and landing on the floor. She always took notice of these wild cards, as they usually carried a significant message.

The Tower landed face upwards and she gasped.

'What is it?' Isis leaned over to get a better look. 'Oh, dear! Not the best card, is it? Even I know that!'

Minerva picked it up and a cold shiver ran through her. A faint cry rang out in her mind and she strained to hear it, to make some sense of it. It was out of her reach and she knew it. She would have to wait.

'No, it's not the best card...' Minerva whispered almost under her breath.

Isis felt the coldness creep into the room. She didn't like it. She watched Minerva as she wrapped the cards back in the cloth and put them to one side, out of the way.

'Not worth turning any more over?'

Minerva shook her head and looked past Isis to the window behind her. 'The Tower is one of the most powerful cards in the deck, Isis, and one of the fastest, too. It signifies change, usually in a big way, and always through some kind of major upheaval. It clears away all the dead wood...' Her voice drifted off.

'What do you see Minerva?'

'I'm not sure that I can or I want to, whatever it is. Sometimes we don't always get the full picture...'

The telephone rang, breaking the tension and Isis breathed a sigh of relief.

'Oh hello, David... Yes, I mean no, I don't mind. Okay... Yes, Isis is here, shall I bring her? I'm sure she'd like to help...' Minerva placed the handset face down on her shoulder. 'David's had a flower delivery, do you fancy coming down with me to the church and arranging them?'

Isis knew what that meant. She'd seen that *refuse at your peril* glare many a time. She nodded and smiled, glad for the change of subject.

'We'll be down in a minute, David,' said Minerva sweetly. 'Yes, okay... Bye.'

'Flower arranging...in the church?' Isis smiled at her friend. 'Whatever next?'

'I have absolutely no idea,' said Minerva, checking herself in the mirror. 'But it'll come soon enough, I'm sure.'

* * *

Ronnie was enjoying the fact that she could still ride. No doubt she'd get to the stage when it would be too uncomfortable, but for now, she relished her time with Bob. Today, they were enjoying a ride out with Kismet and Sophia. The land was well and truly in the grip of winter and a damp mist hung around them as they trotted along the sea wall.

'Even when it's cold like this, it's great to be out, don't you think?' Ronnie turned to her companion.

'Especially along here. I love the wildness of the place... They do, too!' Sophia nodded to both horses as they snorted big clouds of misty steam and the girls laughed.

Ronnie pushed Bob into canter and Kismet bounded forward in quick succession, not wanting to be left behind. It wasn't long before the pair were racing along, caught up in the moment. They were creatures of flight and impulse, running with the herd; hooves and hearts pounding, with only speed on their minds.

On and on they went, the four of them, warriors and steeds chasing the wind along the sea-wall track...fused together as one, the sheer liberty of being alive driving them on. It was intoxicating - adrenalin coursing through every vein - and propelling them along. Fast.

Ronnie didn't see the hole until it was too late. It pulled them down instantly. One minute, they were on the tail of Kismet and Sophia – not quite able to keep up with a thoroughbred more suited to racing than a cob – and the next, they were down the fox hole. It shouldn't have been there, not on the side of the lower ditch, but accidents don't follow sets of rules. They just happen.

Ronnie was thrown sideways and landed with a heavy thud – quick and violent. She lay motionless, stunned by the fall. Bob also landed heavily, but tried to get up just as quickly. Instinct was strong in him to keep going, but not enough to overcome his inability to do so. One front leg succeeded in pulling his great weight up, while the other crumpled underneath him and failed at the attempt. He fell awkwardly again, rolling halfway out of the hole and, with a defiant groan, surrendered to defeat.

Only when Sophia turned to call to Ronnie behind her did she see what had happened. She pulled her mare up with a fierce jerk of the rein, anchoring her weight fully against the horse and after turning sharply, was soon with the fallen horse and rider.

'Ronnie! Ronnie! Are you all right? Ronnie!' Sophia's screams hit the air in desperation as she jumped off Kismet and bent over her friend.

'Can you move? Are you all right, Ron?' She reached out and touched her limp form.

'I think so… Bob…where's Bob?' Croaked Ronnie, straining her head to try and see.

'Oh, thank God you're talking! Can you move, Ron? Can you move at all?'

Sophia turned to see Bob, lying on his side, his head nodding in a pathetic attempt to pull himself up. 'Bob's there, Ron…he's there!' She felt helpless.

'Have you got your phone? *Sophia, have you got your phone?*' Screamed Ronnie when she saw her horse. 'Get help… Ring someone…please…'

Sophia felt for her phone and with one hand rang the stables. It was the first number that came to mind. They'd know what to do.

Ronnie managed to scramble up, but the pain hit her and she bent over sharply. The sheer force of it crushed her in two and she folded like a concertina and finally collapsed, after making it over to Bob's flailing legs. His eyes had rolled back and his breathing was coming in gasps. She didn't make a sound. Nothing would come out.

When he saw her, Bob lifted his head and heaved his great body up and off the ground. It was a desperate attempt to cling to the familiar, a struggle to overcome the unknown. Instinct is a powerful force, but love is stronger and no man or beast escapes either.

Ronnie got out of the way just in time, before she saw Bob's leg. Before she realized he couldn't put any weight on it. Before she collapsed into darkness.

9

Hospitals and Heaven

By the time the vet arrived on the scene, Ronnie was coming round under a blanket. Poor Sophia wasn't sure if this was a good thing or not. It was pretty clear to her what Bob's problem was, and she knew that Ronnie had seen it too – although how much she'd remember, after falling so heavily, Sophia couldn't tell. But it was obvious to anyone with even a basic eye for the anatomical make-up of a horse: this one had broken its leg. The fetlock hung limply, and at an odd angle. It didn't look good.

Gail Milton, the yard proprietor, had known exactly what to do, thank god, because Sophia hadn't. She had eased the situation straight way, with her practical show of calm efficiency, and taken everything into hand. Ronnie had been gently lifted into the four-wheel drive, where she'd fainted again and they'd covered her with a blanket while Gail had quickly assessed Bob and rung the vet. Fortunately, he would be able to get straight there, as this part of the sea wall was accessible via a back lane.

Gail didn't hold out much hope; she had seen it all before.

She remembered when Sally, her faithful old mare, had done the same thing in the field. She'd found her, and was glad it had been her and no-one else.

It was a messy sight.

Any of the other girls would not have handled the situation as well, she was sure. But she'd stayed calm and called the vet and nodded when he'd given his verdict, and she had held old Sally there in the field while he had gone to fetch his case. She'd spoken to her and stroked her neck and told her not to worry and that everything was going to be all right. And when the vet came back, she had stood stock still by Sally's head and kept her hand on the warm neck until the mare had gone down. She had phoned the meat man and directed him with a curt smile to the field and the great ugly mound of horse flesh that had been Sally, and watched as he covered her in chains and hauled her on to the back of his lorry.

She had even managed a polite thank you when he had pressed a wad of paper notes into her hand as he left, chains rattling from the inside, where Sally was. She had stood at the end of the drive and watched the back of the lorry as it rumbled out, and then walked back to the yard and carried on her day as usual. It wasn't until John had come in off the fields that evening and they'd had dinner and she had washed up and cleared up and checked the yards and followed John up the stairs and into bed, where he held her gently... Only then did she say a silent goodbye to her four-legged friend, as she buried her face in the pillow.

* * *

'I'm going to have to do it here, Gail, I'm afraid,' said the vet, after a very quick examination.

'Yes, I know, Mark,' she said. 'Do you mind waiting until after they've gone?' She nodded to the ambulance coming towards them down the track and then to the four-wheel drive.

'No, of course not,' he called back as he made his way to his car.

Ronnie was still unconscious when the ambulance took off, with her and Sophia strapped to the inside. Sophia had been assured by Gail that everything would be taken care of. She had phoned for one of the experienced girls to come and ride Kismet back, and Gail said she would see to everything else as well. There was no need to worry – and it was best to get themselves checked out, especially Ronnie, as she'd fallen badly.

You have no idea! Thought Sophia, but she was grateful. Mrs Milton seemed to know just what to do. Sophia leaned across the ambulance interior and reached for Ronnie's hand as the engine rumbled into life.

'Any allergies or other conditions that you know of?' The paramedic woman asked, as she draped another blanket over Ronnie.

'Yes...she's pregnant,' said Sophia. 'About six months, I think.'

Immediately, the paramedic lifted the blanket and examined Ronnie further.

'Is everything all right?' Sophia said, gripping on to Ronnie's hand.

'Hard to tell in here, but we'll get her sorted out as soon as we can – not to worry.'

No, of course not, thought Sophia, *nothing to worry about at all. She's just had her horse put down and doesn't know it yet – never mind, eh?*

'But she's okay, isn't she? Ronnie's okay?'

'All vitals normal, considering,' said the paramedic, narrowing her eyes at her watch. 'Obviously, she's in shock at the moment but...they'll be able to give her a thorough examination soon.'

And that was it for the rest of the journey. Silence. More checks. More silence. But Sophia didn't mind. It gave her time to gather her thoughts. What next? Should she ring Minerva or would Gail do that? She would ring Gail and find out.

She felt in her coat pocket for her phone. But it wasn't there.

* * *

A church was the most unlikely of places to hear the opening bars of Green Day's *American Idiot* – but, with Minerva in the place, anything was possible. She was halfway up a ladder with an armful of lilies when her mobile's rebellious ringtone belted out across the stone walls. With no way of reaching for it and feeling contrary, she waited as the crashing guitars boomed out a second time, giving the church the full effect of one of her favourite musical masterpieces. Glancing down, she caught a look of utter disdain from Isis, just as David walked through the doors with a plate of sandwiches from the vicarage.

She really ought to answer it.

'Oh hello, Gail. Yes, it's Minerva...'

David and Isis gravitated towards a frowning Minerva as she slowly descended on to the front-row pew, dragging a hand through her wild, red hair.

'So, where is she now?... At the hospital... I see...and Bob?' Minerva bent forward and rested her elbows on her knees, staring hard at the floor. 'Thank you, Gail. I appreciate that... Yes, I'll let you know... Thanks.'

An absurd and fleeting thought occurred to Minerva: that, of all the places to receive bad news, a church was probably not a bad one - and for that - she was thankful.

There was something oddly comforting about it. She wasn't alone either, which helped. David lightly touched her shoulder and Isis sat down beside her.

'It's the stables. I mean that was the stables,' Minerva said, in a hushed, robotic tone. 'It was Gail. She said there's been an accident with Ronnie and Bob... Poor Bob's broken a leg, badly... The vet is...there at the moment...'

'And Ronnie?' said Isis. 'Where's Ronnie?'

'My Goddess, yes – Ronnie... She's on her way to hospital... She's okay, she thinks...but... Your car, David, where's your car?' Minerva looked at David.

'Come on, both of you,' he said, taking some keys out of his pocket. 'It's just outside.'

Minerva got up slowly and followed them both out of the church in deep thought. Her hand flew to her throat with a gasp as the image of the tarot's Tower flashed into her mind and she watched it crash into the sea...

She knew it would fall. But not this quickly.

* * *

Minerva wasn't keen on hospitals. Strangely enough, she'd much rather have been in church. Perhaps being in a hospital with David wasn't so bad. It was certainly better than being in a hospital with Isis. The journey had soothed Minerva's nerves; David's driving tended to have a calming effect on her. However, Isis did not respond in the same way, and by the time they arrived at the Shockton General, she was like a cat on hot bricks. It was driving Minerva mad.

'Isis, do you want to stay in the car?' she asked, predicting trouble.

'No, of course not... Oh...do you want me to?' Isis stopped, halfway out of the car.

'Only if you are going to continue in this manner...'

'What manner, Minerva?' Isis looked wounded.

Minerva immediately regretted what she'd said. 'Oh look, it doesn't... I mean, I'm sorry... I'm just worried, that's all...'

'Shall we go, ladies?' David stepped between them, edging carefully forwards, and they walked slowly in silence, between the multitudes of cars, towards the main building.

'Where will she be?' Minerva sounded like a lost child.

'I'd say A and E will be our best bet – for starters, anyway,' said David, taking her arm and steering her gently forwards.

He signalled to them both to wait while he went to the reception area to locate Ronnie. Minerva was beginning to shiver and Isis was fidgeting madly as they kept their eyes fixed on David.

Fortunately, they didn't have to wait too long which was just as well as Minerva's intolerance now extended to a room full of casualties, leaving Isis and her jittery nerves all but forgotten.

They moved to the edge of their seats as David returned. He had that heavenly look about him and, in that moment, Minerva saw something special in this man she'd grown very fond of in a short space of time.

'She's in Maternity,' he said.

'Oh my Goddess... Does that mean she's...?' Minerva panicked.

'They couldn't tell me any more. Come on...'

David took off at a brisk walk and led the way down long

corridors and through seemingly endless doorways until they reached the Maternity Ward.

'Ah yes, she had an emergency caesarean and is in the special baby care unit just down there.' The young woman behind a desk told them as she pointed down another corridor.

Minerva couldn't speak. She just followed David as he glided in front of them, in total control. Isis shuffled along behind them, her skirt swishing loudly and oddly out of rhythm with the scuff of her sandals against the polished floors.

Another set of doors and three hand cleansers later, and they were there.

'We'll wait here, Minerva,' David said quietly. 'I've a feeling they'll only allow you to go in.'

He was right.

Minerva was led into the main area, encased in glass partitions. This time, she followed a large, bustling bottom in pale blue check, which took her into a side room and spoke to her in soft tones. She couldn't take it all in. She caught words like 'baby' and 'surgery' and 'incubator' in snatches, as she stood rather helplessly, looking at the bed.

Ronnie was lying there and, next to her, was a small, see-through case, with a mass of tubes attached to it. Inside was a doll, she was sure of it. It was no bigger than her hand - well, maybe slightly; David's hand, perhaps.

She drew a sharp intake of breath and silenced it with her hand.

'Ronnie…' she whispered, 'can you hear me?'

'Mum, is that you?'

The nurse had said she was still quite drowsy with painkillers and that it could only be a good thing, considering. Minerva was dreading telling her. Sophia had passed on the awful news and it was now up to her to tell Ronnie.

She felt like the Grim Reaper.

I won't have to tell her just now, she thought. *It can wait till tomorrow, at least.*

'Bob...where's Bob, Mum? Is he all right? What did the vet say?'

Minerva pulled up a chair and sat down beside her daughter. She picked up her hand and noticed how cold it was, in spite of the warm room. A needle plastered at an odd angle stuck out of the back of it, and a plastic bracelet hung around her white wrist. She squeezed it and met Ronnie's stark gaze searching her face for an answer.

'Ron...I...'

There were no more words. There was no need. Ronnie knew. She could tell by the feel of her mother's hand as it found hers, and the slow release of pressure told her more than any useless words could. She knew what it meant. Something bad had happened. It was the same squeeze Minerva had given her when Dad had left.

Never coming back.

The sound came from the back of her throat and stopped before it got to her lips. It stuck there and she opened her mouth, but nothing happened.

In that moment...her world stopped.

* * *

Everyone had gone. She was on her own...apart from the Small Thing in the box. Every time she moved, a sharp pain seared its way across the lower part of her stomach. It seemed to burn her from the inside, raging at her, reminding her.

You have paid a price.

A price for what? She traced it back in her mind and it always came back to the same place. The same person.

Joe.

If it hadn't been for Joe, then none of this would have happened. None of it. She wouldn't have been upset over Posh Bird and got drunk and got pregnant and lost Bob. But it wasn't that simple was it? She couldn't blame Joe. He wasn't to know how she felt and, even if he did, he wasn't responsible for her feelings. She was.

The buck stopped with her. It was her fault.

She looked at the mass of tubes next to her and looked away again. She was empty. There was nothing there. Just a hole. And pain. And every time she remembered, it hurt more. And *that* was the living reminder of her loss. What had been and gone and was no more.

Bob Marley, her lovely Bob... How would she cope? She hadn't even been there for him or *with* him. She couldn't go any further in her mind. Imagination is a potent source of power. It makes things real. That's its job. She couldn't make it work forwards, only backwards. She wanted out.

They gave her morphine and it helped. It brought her nothingness. And she drifted in between the worlds and found herself willing to go further...as far away from herself as she could. She willed herself to be anywhere but where she was...to be anyone else but who she was.

So she slept.

The nurses came in and out. They made encouraging noises, patted and humoured her. They tried to interest her in the Small Thing beside her. She told them about the pain and asked them to stop it. And they produced needles and tablets and told her it would go, which it did, for a while. But it came back…every time she remembered. Every time she looked at the Small Thing. Every time she looked at herself.

Sleeping helped and she decided in that room that she would quite like to sleep forever.

It seemed like a good idea for a bad life.

* * *

'But she doesn't want to see *anyone*, David. She barely speaks to me and has no interest at all in the baby.' Minerva was desperate.

'These things take time, Minerva.'

'*These things*! These *things* are my daughter and what is happening to her. These things are not one of your *all things bright and bloody beautiful*, David. These things are desperado stakes. This is all that is lost and is no more. This is not bloody heaven, you know – this is bloody *hell*!'

Minerva was shouting and David was glad of the open air and the quiet woodland track they'd taken for their walk. She could shout all she wanted, for all he cared. It would do her good. Get it out of her system. It wasn't easy, but he was a patient man and also a smitten one. He could forgive the drama queen. He could in fact, when he thought about it, forgive Minerva anything…

He slipped an arm around the small of her back. 'Life can strike cruel blows sometimes, Minerva, it's true. People fall down. Ronnie has probably fallen as far as she ever has or will do again. And it's just as hard to watch someone suffer, if not more so, because feeling helpless is a futile experience. This is hard for you, I know, but life is a process that requires time.

Ronnie has to digest what's happened. None of it will be easy, but she'll get through it...really she will.'

'But how long? It's been weeks, David! She's supposed to be coming home tomorrow *with* the baby, who is still very tiny and needs a lot of care. So far, the hospital's been wonderful and the nurses have been doing it all. But now...' Panic and palpitations didn't go well together.

'Minerva,' he stopped and took both her hands in his, 'you love your daughter and you love your granddaughter...'

'As romantic as it all sounds David, *love* is not the only thing that's required here. We need a lot more than that.'

'Of course you do, but the help is there for you, isn't it?'

'Well...yes, the midwife will come every day for another few weeks at least...and the health visitor...'

'And you'll be there...'

'Well, of course I'll be there... What do you mean?'

'Then she'll have all the support she needs: medical help, plus TLC from you.'

Minerva went to interrupt, but he carried on: '*You*, of course, will have myself and Isis to help out – so please, Minerva – have some faith. Ronnie will, I'm sure, come round in her own time. If there are any more serious issues that arise and she needs further help, then, again, I'm sure it will be available to her. What will *not* help is you worrying about it all.'

She looked at him and sighed. He was right. She knew he was right.

He pulled her to him and she fell against his chest as the strong arms went around her.

'I don't know what I would honestly do without you, really I don't,' she said.

'You would cope, I'm sure,' he laughed. 'But of course I'm

happy to be of service... Madam.' He bowed deeply to the ground.

'Perhaps we ought to be getting back,' said Minerva. 'I think it's a bit nippy for outdoor sex, don't you?'

He gave a throaty chuckle as they turned for home. 'That's what I like about you, Minerva...'

'And what would that be, David...?'

'You're honest...and...to-the-point. I like that in a woman.'

Minerva gave a wicked laugh. 'Well, I can't really see the point in being anything else, can you?'

'Absolutely not,' said David, quickening his step.

* * *

Minerva was making the most of the last few hours with the house to herself. There was nothing like a deadline to focus the mind. Somehow, the knowledge of a small window of time added a spark to the already smouldering flame of passion inside her...a flame that only a man could ignite.

David could light her fire any time, but she thought she'd play it down as much as she could get away with – she didn't want to appear overly keen. After their walk in the woods, she told him she was busy for the rest of the day, but she would cook dinner that night and he could bring his guitar, if he pleased. She hoped that wasn't the only instrument he would be willing to show her, and amused herself with the idea of an evening of fun and frolicking with the vicar...

By the Goddess, she needed it.

She believed that success was in the preparation, and decided to dedicate the final hours before David's arrival to some serious sex magic. She thought it through carefully...didn't they already have the romantic ingredient? Of course they did. But the sex? It appeared to have eluded them so far, which was hardly surprising, as life had taken a rather sombre turn of late. Nothing dampened the ardour more did it?

Not for much longer, she thought.

She was sure that he felt the same. Well, almost. That is, as sure as one could be with a man of the cloth. But just a little help in the aphrodisiac department wouldn't do any harm at all. With a wicked grin, she whistled loudly and unashamedly out of tune as she delved into her spell book once again for some magical enlightenment.

* * *

Isis was pleased with herself. She didn't often get the chance to buy presents for babies and she wanted to show off her bundle of pink-and-fluffy things. And Minerva must be in; the lights were on in Crafty Cottage.

She waited for ages, but no-one answered. Perhaps she'd just popped out?

As she made her way back down the path, it was hard to ignore the loud thud from an upstairs window, where Minerva was waving frantically.

Isis let herself in. 'Minerva…*what* are you doing?'

Minerva was coming down the stairs with a towel. But she wasn't wrapped in it. She was holding it up in front of her and was just visible from the neck upwards and the knees downwards.

'I'm air-drying,' said Minerva, seriously.

'You're what?'

'I'm air-drying to radiate the botanical and magical powers

of my *seduction bath*. Cinnamon, cloves, coriander seeds and cardamom. They're all in it, you know.'

'They're all in the bath?'

'Not actually in it, Isis, no. You pour boiling water over them and then add the *tincture* to the bath. Immerse and bathe for an hour and hey presto – the ultimate love potion and aphrodisiac! Then, after careful *air-drying*, anoint with liberal amounts of *Follow Me Boy* oil. And if that doesn't guarantee a night of erotic abandonment – tailor made, of course – then I don't know what will.'

'And, pray tell, what is in this *Follow Me Boy* oil?' asked Isis.

'Dried damiana and catnip…'

'What! Sounds an odd combination to me, Minerva, are you sure?'

'Can you get the book and read it to me, Ice? Perhaps I should check.'

'No, you're right,' said Isis, scanning the page. 'Powder the ingredients together and add to sweet almond oil…finally adding any essential oils of one's choice.'

Minerva managed a polite chuckle. 'Oh good. Well, I've already prepared it, so that's all right.'

'Where did you get the catnip from?' asked Isis.

'Where you think?' said Minerva, pointing to Lucifer's basket, where the remains of a butchered cotton mouse lay in the corner.

'Are you sure that's the right stuff? Is it the right type of catnip?' She didn't like the sound of it, but Minerva was adamant. 'Oh for God's sake, Ice, it must be. I'm not about to start faffing around now, changing things. According to the book, it will draw men like flies.'

Or cats like Lucifer, thought Isis. It didn't bear thinking about.

'Well, I won't keep you from your evening then, Minerva. I only hope it works and that your night of passion is hot, steamy and memorable!'

'Yes, absolutely; I do hope so. Ronnie comes home tomorrow, so this is my last chance to net David on home ground, so to speak.'

'You mean you haven't already?'

'Actually no, Isis, and is that such a bad thing? David has been the perfect gentleman, but enough is enough, if you ask me. A girl can only take so much of so little.'

'Look out David, then! Will he wear his dog collar, do you think?'

'I sincerely hope he won't be wearing anything at all, not if I can help it,' said Minerva. 'Now if you don't mind, Isis, I have some important business to attend to... Let yourself out!'

She retreated backwards up the stairs behind the towel and disappeared before Isis had a chance to reply. Clearly *nothing* was going to stop her and why should it? Minerva deserved some fun in what had been a considerably un-funny time of late.

I'd do the very same myself, thought Isis, carefully placing the beautifully wrapped baby clothes on the side table before leaving.

10

Catnip and Cleavages

Was it right for a vicar to look like Johnny Depp? Minerva was past caring as she tried hard not to appear too fixated on the vision before her... Drooling like a dog was not very becoming.

David pushed his plate politely away from him and finished his wine. 'Compliments to the chef. That was delicious,' he said, dabbing his mouth with his serviette. The Celtic knot edging fluttered against his dark goatee beard and Minerva couldn't help noticing how his eyes glittered in the candlelight. Not that she minded one bit, but it struck her as odd that a man of God could look so wickedly devilish.

'Good,' said Minerva, rather abruptly, 'I'm glad you enjoyed it. Could you taste the saffron?'

'Was it in the rice?' he asked.

'It was in everything,' she murmured seductively. 'It's got...shall we say...certain qualities.'

She smiled slowly over the rim of her glass at him as one dark, devilish eyebrow shot up at her. It was pure synchronicity. 'Oh, I see! You wouldn't have an ulterior motive, I suppose?' 'More wine, vicar?' She reached across for the bottle, feeling his eyes on her. 'Go on, be a devil!'

'Fancy bringing him up,' he laughed. 'If anyone's going to come between a Witch and a vicar, I suppose it would have to be him!'

'Well, funny you should say that. In the tarot, he's a sexy beast, you know: the embodiment of lust and desire...' She leaned towards him. 'Is that allowed...vicar?'

He lowered his gaze to the top of her low-cut dress. She had mastered the art of leaning forwards to display her best assets in the most alluring way. And it was working. He couldn't take his eyes off her *or* her assets.

Encouraged by his response so far, Minerva was pleased: the evening was having the desired effect... *She* was having the desired effect. She sent a few silent words of praise to the Goddess and stood up. Without waiting for a reply, she picked up the wine and their glasses and made her way to the sofa, stopping on the way to discreetly add another ten drops of ylang ylang to the oil burner. It was a sweet and sensual aroma, full of aphrodisiac qualities – and, although the evening was clearly going in the right direction, one couldn't be too presumptuous.

Minerva was not leaving a stone unturned.

'Shall we make ourselves more comfortable?' She gestured dramatically to the purple velour cushions, feeling rather proud of herself.

'It certainly seems like a good idea,' said a smiling David, as he joined her.

Everything was going according to plan.

The atmosphere was electrifying and alive with anticipation. It tingled and permeated the walls themselves. David thought how cave-like and primeval it was, just like Minerva. Illuminating a wooden pentacle here and a brass Goddess there, the soft glow of candle flames glimmered around the room.

The red candles for seduction, Minerva thought, were an obvious choice – and, with all the magical intent she could muster up – she'd carved a word with the end of her nail file along the side of each one. Because of its simplicity, candle magic had always been a favourite of hers. However, one should never underestimate the power of it.

Simple, according to Minerva, was usually best.

She just hoped David wouldn't notice *what* she'd etched so carefully onto each candle in large letters... *SEX* was not exactly a word of discretion, just as subtlety was of little use in the ways of magic – that was, if one wished it to work.

Minerva had never been so focused. The earthy sounds of her new shamanic album filled the room with its pulsating drum and driving rhythms. Tonight was not the time for the titillating strings of the celestial spheres, she chuckled inwardly. Deep down and tantric was a much better place to be.

As they settled on the sofa, Minerva was careful to position herself so that the amount of flesh exposed was as tasteful as it was seductive. She didn't want to come across like a brazen hussy (although, absurdly, she was enjoying feeling like one) and neither did she want to appear prudish. It was all about getting the right balance.

'Is it too warm in here?' she asked, willing herself *not* to give in to the dreaded hot flush and prickly heat that threatened beneath the surface of her clammy skin.

'I don't think so; are you okay?' He couldn't take his eyes off her...glistening like a Goddess before him.

Such a considerate man, she thought.

144

'Yes,' she lied. 'Are you?' 'What's that smell?'

He reached into his pocket and for a moment she wondered what on earth was in there – she wasn't quite ready for the bedroom yet – but was relieved when he produced a handkerchief embossed with gold holy crosses. She doubted if God would save him now, when a fit of violent sneezing proceeded to drown out the pulsating sounds of the shaman's drum. And as poor David pressed his hanky to his face, it turned a darker shade of beetroot.

'I think it's that thing over there...' He pointed to the oil burner.

'Oh, I am sorry,' said Minerva. 'Are you allergic?'

'Only to certain scents, but that's one of them. It's ylang ylang, isn't it?'

She nodded.

'Yes, I thought so. My grandmother used to burn it. Had the same effect on me then...'

'Oh, I'm so sorry!' she gushed. 'David... shall we go upstairs?'

'I thought you'd never ask,' he said, in between the endless trumpeting, nasal blasts. 'Who do you think I need to ask...God?'

'Do you think he'd approve?' she asked, taking his hand and pulling him up the stairs.

'Wholeheartedly!' he sniffed. 'How could anyone not approve of you Minerva? You're an angel...in disguise, maybe...but an angel, none the less.'

'Well, I'm glad you can see beneath the surface,' she said, peeling off the clingier-than-ever top, now soaked in the sweat of a hot flush.

'Oh, I can see, all right,' he said, 'and I'm *liking* what I see.'

However, there was something they both *didn't* see... Lucifer, curled up in a tight, black ball at the end of Minerva's bed...and so far, undisturbed.

Until now. That was, until every piece of outer clothing had been removed and cast hastily on the floor. And until they had dived feverishly under the billowing duvet covers...

It was then, he pounced. It could have been worse: he could have gone for both of them; but he was only interested in Minerva. He was frantic. He was possessed. He jumped between them and all over her in a most bizarre fashion, as if he was playing with some toy.

A catnip toy.

'What the... Lucifer...get off, you rogue!' cried Minerva, tussling with the beast.

'What's the matter with him?' David's muffled voice came from underneath the duvet, which he'd managed to pin around himself. Cat claws in such close proximity were not what he'd had in mind.

'I think it's the catnip!' she said, bravely fending off the crazed cat.

'What? Cat toys in the bed?'

'No! *I'm* in the bed!'

'I *know* you're in the bed, Minerva!' David's exasperated cries rang around the bedroom. '*What* in heaven's name are you talking about?'

'I used the catnip in his toy for the *Follow Me Boy* Oil... It's a *spell*,' she said impatiently, while managing to grab Lucifer by the scruff of the neck.

David looked at her - this flame haired, wild woman, plugged into the national grid, skin beaded with sweat, reddened with bloody scratches and not a stitch on - was a sight to behold. A goddess on fire.

'A spell?' he said. 'Well, it's worked, Minerva... You've got me well and truly under it.' And he didn't mean the duvet.

'Are you sure?' said Minerva, looking sheepish.

'As the Lord is my witness,' said a flustered but deadly serious David.

It hadn't all been for nothing then, thought Minerva, stumbling down the stairs to throw Lucifer out and bolting the cat flap firmly behind him.

* * *

Ronnie had been home for weeks and it wasn't getting any easier. The Small Thing was an intrusion into her world...a world shrunk to the size of a baby.

It was a constant reminder of the shadow cast over her life; every day proclaiming: *YOU WILL NOT FORGET!* in loud wails – until eventually, Ronnie picked her up without saying a word and the Small Thing would stop. It became an automatic reflex and Ronnie drifted from one day to the next in this forced, robotic role called motherhood.

But it did nothing to satisfy the longing she still had for her beloved horse. In fact, it was the poorest substitute she could ever imagine and she spent what seemed like hours staring past the tiny bundle and into the empty space beyond. The Small Thing did not fill the empty shell that she had become. All it did was irritate and wear her down with sleep deprivation and constant demands. The one saving grace was her mother. Without her help, she would have crumbled.

'Ronnie, darling, have you thought of one yet?' Minerva asked her one morning as they ate breakfast together.

'Thought of what?' asked Ronnie, chewing her toast slowly

and staring out of the window.

'A name, of course! I can't believe this poor child still doesn't have one.' She looked at her sleeping granddaughter in the Moses basket beside her.

'No.'

Minerva was getting tired of these one-syllable answers from Ronnie. She was being as patient as she could, but it was a virtue wearing thin. She had listened to David and taken on board everything that he'd said…all the good advice. She was trying, she really was. But Ronnie would not snap out of it. This aftermath of fate's cruel blow, this darkest of moods that had descended upon her, seemed to have her in its grip and was not letting go. She could at least make some kind of effort to *let it go*…but no.

Minerva didn't want to push it, but it was worrying her. The child needed a name. Without it, she was undefined. A nothing.

She didn't deserve it.

She went to the bookshelf, came back and placed a book firmly on the table in front of Ronnie, who glanced down lazily at the cover: *The Goddess Path*.

'You might get some inspiration from that…all the names of every Goddess and what they mean,' sighed Minerva. 'Both of us are in there; wouldn't it be lovely if she was, too? I'm sure she is…*somewhere*.'

Ronnie looked at her mother. She would do it for her, if nothing else. She leafed through the well-thumbed pages in alphabetical order and stopped at *M*. There it was. A perfect name. She turned the book round and pointed it out to her mother. 'That's it…that's her name.'

Minerva caught the hint of darkness in her voice before she

saw the word, so it came as no surprise.

'Morrigan!' she cried, 'Goddess of battle, war and death. Oh, Ronnie, are you sure? Is it fair on the poor thing?'

'Is anything fair, Mum? I think it suits her. Very apt, don't you think? She represents the circle of life, and isn't death part of that? It's what you've always told me – and she *was* born out of it, after all. However, Morrigan is the patroness of priestesses and Witches, so surely that makes up for it.'

Minerva thought something had stirred in Ronnie. This was the first time she'd seen any kind of life in her for what had seemed like an age. She mustn't knock it. And besides it was true: the forces of death and darkness were as much a part of life as were the living and the light. She had brought her daughter up to know that – and now that she was experiencing it, how could they deny its existence? This tiny thing who had entered their lives was right here to remind them.

How poignant was this divine timing of the great Goddess?

'Rhiannon, I named you myself, and it is only right you should name your daughter. I think it's actually an incredibly beautiful name. Such power and strength!
She will grow into that power, just as we have grown into ours and will ever continue to do so for the rest of our lives. This is an important moment...' She stopped and breathed in deeply, 'The maiden, mother and the crone... The Triple Goddess! We are as one! Can you feel the magical energy? It's alive! It's palpable!' Minerva flung her arms wide and looked around in wonder.

Trust her mother to turn it into some big deal, thought Ronnie.

It was only a name.

* * *

Isis needed some fresh air. Cold it may have been, but wrapped up in her latest charity shop number, she hardly felt the bitter January wind as it whipped around the fake fur and escorted her away from Crafty Cottage and towards home. Two hours of Minerva was enough under the best of circumstances, but two hours of listening to her steamy stories of new-found love and the heavenly David was more than she could bear.

Isis was quite sure that getting hot under his dog collar must be a very private affair, and not one he would appreciate being so publicly flaunted by a fired-up and theatrical Minerva. But there was no telling her once she had the drama queen's bit between her teeth; it was about as much use as an ashtray on a motorbike, Derek would say. And, given her ex-husband's opinion of her friend, it could easily have been the very description he would use for her. How odd!

However, getting hot under her hair-piece was usually the sign for Isis to leave, and prompted by a glaring Minerva, who Isis was sure had the power to make it slide and topple – she was up and off when it did. There was only so much a girl could take, especially when Minerva was not only narrating but demonstrating at times – in quite graphic detail – what they were getting up to in the bedroom, the Morris and even in the woods of all places. *Whatever next*, thought Isis, stopping herself as an image of the church and its altar arose on the screen of her mind in full Technicolor. That was the problem with being highly strung: one was saddled with a highly imaginative thought process, which behaved like a runaway train at times…and the only solution was to run.

She picked up speed – and her bright, wrap around skirt –

and with great gusto, marched headlong into the facing wind, which had picked up with great ferocity.

Ronnie squinted beneath her woolly hat at the colourful, whirling figure coming towards her. Seeing Isis, caught up in wind and fur, with head down and hair-piece at an extreme right- angle, she couldn't help but smile. Just the sight of Isis lifted her spirits.

She was a watery rainbow in a gloomy sky: fragile and lovely.

'Hey, Isis! Looks like you're on a mission…'

'Oh, Ronnie,' said a startled Isis. 'You made me jump! I didn't see you…and oh yes, a mission indeed…' She laughed nervously. 'What have you named her?' She peered into the pram, against the wind. 'Your mother did tell me…but then she was telling me a lot of other things, too, and…well, you know I get a little distracted and confused at times.'

'Yeah, well, that's not hard with Mum around, is it? She's enough to distract anyone,' said Ronnie, 'especially at the moment…vicarly love and all that. What do you reckon, then?' Ronnie winked at an embarrassed-looking Isis.

'Does she have a name yet?' asked Isis, staring with great intensity into the pram. 'I didn't catch it.'

'What…?' said Ronnie, looking at the Small Thing. 'Oh yes, it's Morrigan, Goddess of battle and death…and *sex* of course!'

Isis looked up with a start. 'Oh!' she said. 'Well… I'm sure she will grow into it, in the nicest possible way.'

'Actually, it also means 'Sea Queen',' said Ronnie, softening. 'Do you like it now, Isis?'

Isis smiled, 'Ronnie, she's an absolute dear and, whatever her name, I'm sure she will be just perfect.' Isis was under the Small Thing's spell already. 'Baby Morrigan it is! Let me know if you ever need a babysitter, Ronnie… I'll be only too happy to oblige.'

And with that, Isis hurried away, blowing a huge kiss behind her.

'Oh thanks, Isis – you're a star woman!' shouted Ronnie, the first pangs of guilt setting in. Why had she done that? It was awful, really; poor, undeserving Isis…so easy to wind up. But she could see why her mother did it…it was too tempting not to.

Isis felt decidedly better for their brief encounter. She loved babies. Maybe if Derek hadn't been such a miserable cad, she might have had one of her own before he'd gone and scampered off with the Molly Maid. Perhaps all was not lost: she still had time. Lots of women had babies in their forties – forty-three wasn't so old, was it?

Anyway, how good it was to see Ronnie recovering – *and about time too,* she thought… But how very much like her mother she'd become.

* * *

The wind was getting stronger and Ronnie spotted some shelter up ahead, in the form of the village bus stop. It looked rather lonely with just the surrounding farmland for company, so she thought she'd venture inside with the Small Thing and take the opportunity for a smoke.

It struck her suddenly, like a blow from behind. Grief has a habit of doing that. There she was; in a bus stop with a baby on the very route she would have taken with her beloved horse! It was him she should be with: Bob, with his warm breath and soft nose. Bob and the smell of hay and leather and saddle-soap and stables. Her Bob.

She couldn't even light her cigarette for the tears and the shaking. Her whole body seemed to convulse into a heaving and sobbing she had no control over. She should be with him, not this Small Thing in a pram. She allowed herself to imagine for a moment what it would be like…what it felt like to be dead. And the strangest part was, it didn't frighten her – she felt no fear. In fact, it appealed in more ways than she thought it would. What if…?

'Now, that's not healthy thinking, is it, dear warrior soul?'

She turned suddenly, in the direction of the voice behind her. In the field, just a few feet from the bus stop, was the Hermit. 'Why do you call me a warrior?' she asked, between sobs.

'Because you are strong and feisty and now, more than ever, you need to draw on your power. It will only weaken you to think of leaving the earth plane before your time on it is over. Turn to the living.' He gestured to the Small Thing.

'Well, let me tell you, old man: I don't really feel like it so much anymore!'

There was desperation in her voice as she clung to the words and the side of the pram for support.

'Are you not the mother of this child?' he boomed at her. 'She has been put in your care for good reason, which will reveal itself in the fullness of time. While you may think you are not worthy of motherhood, she does not deserve your thoughts about her own unworthiness. She has chosen you before coming to this time and place…and YOU, dear warrior, have a sacred contract to fulfil!'

He stamped his bent and gnarled staff on the hard earth.

'SHE was the reason I lost my horse! If it hadn't been…'

The Hermit's thunderous tones echoed around the small enclosure. 'You are erroneous in your assumption of the circumstances surrounding her birth. It is true, it was preceded by a passing and your loss is great; this we know and understand...'

'Who's 'we'?' said Ronnie. 'You mean there are more of you?'

'I'm afraid so,' he smiled at her. 'There are many where I come from. The unseen and magical realms house the guides and guardians of old, the Ancients Ones, ready to help when there is a need. We move and live beyond the veil, and our work is important, in measures you cannot conceive, until you have experienced for yourself the subtlety of those worlds.'

Ronnie thought for a moment. 'Then how come I can see you now? How can I hear you and *understand* you if I am not *experiencing* that world now?'

The Hermit laughed. 'Aha...the spark of awareness! You are able to see and hear because, through your finer senses, you have a natural capacity to experience my world. It is a gift, an opportunity to learn and grow and to eventually help others. It is knowledge and power. But with power comes responsibility. And this, young warrior soul, is your lesson at this time. It hangs upon your shoulders like a heavy weight and you feel it keenly, but only because you fight it and think it is not yours to carry.

The last time we met, you were struggling with a choice, and now that decision has been made for you but there is no blame...to any party.' He looked at the pram. 'Or to yourself. There is only acceptance. When you give up the struggle of denial, life becomes easier, dear soul. This is the way of the warrior: the battle is always with the self. Defending and arming yourself with the knowledge to proceed on your journey is the key to living fully. You know this.'

His words washed over Ronnie in soothing waves and she

felt the burden of heavy emotion slipping away. She looked up at the magical being and felt an awesome peace.

'Thank you,' she said quietly. 'And I'm sorry if I was rude... I...'

He said nothing, only raising a hand towards her, in what appeared to be a blessing. She didn't know *how* she knew it, only that she did. And trying to figure it all out was futile - she was completely drained.

But, walking home she felt something coming back – a small glimmer of hope returning. She looked up at the land and sky around her, and down at the Small Thing in front of her. It was a comfort to know that although she felt close to the edge of a large black hole, it might not be as bad as she thought. Magic appeared at the edges of things, her mother said.

And right now, it seemed closer than ever.

11

Wobbly Weekends and Snowdrops

Minerva smiled at the Two of Cups as she turned it over…to savour these magical moments was always a joy.

'Good lord, Minerva – is there ever a time you don't turn to those cards?' asked David, fastening his dog collar.

'Just checking in with them…' Minerva planted a kiss on his ruffled hair and noticed his ponytail had come undone. 'It aways helps to confirm the situation.'

'Do you really feel the need to?' He continued to straighten his attire and make himself as presentable as any decent chap could at two o'clock in the afternoon in a vicarage.

'Not as much as I feel the need for your God-like self.' She flashed her green cat's eyes at him, while buttoning up her top.

David laughed. 'Well, the card must be a good one,' he said. 'You have that look about you.'

The cat that got the cream, he thought.

'Oh, and that's *nothing* to do with you, vicar, I suppose!' Minerva threw her wild, red mane back and laughed up at the ceiling. 'Aha… It seems we had an audience!' She pointed to the angelic figures, beautifully plastered around each light fitting. 'Why, a heavenly host, no less… Should we have asked them first?'

'Asking the angels couldn't be further from my thoughts when captivated by your mystica charms, Minerva… You're quite the loveliest distraction a man could hope for.'

He bent to kiss her, before taking the tarot card and examining it.

It pleased her that he was interested in her passions, and not just passionate about her body. It added another dimension to their relationship, something else to talk about. She was tired of men who had little to occupy them, other than their own carnal desires. A couple needed something to fall back on, a foundation to build upon – otherwise it could, and invariably did, collapse in a post-coital heap and shrivel up and die.

She didn't want that to happen with David. He was far too good to let go and besides, they understood each other and had such fun. What did it really matter who they worshipped anyway? As far as she was concerned, he was her God and she was his Goddess, a balance of equals. All other forms of deity paled into insignificance in comparison.

'So tell me,' said David, 'what does this mean…this Two of Cups?'

Minerva hesitated. 'How about you tell me, for a change? Won't do any harm to remind yourself of what your grandmother taught you will it?'

David squinted as he studied the card, holding it up to the light. Surely he didn't need to ask the angels, thought Minerva.

'Can you pass me my glasses, please?' he asked, without looking up.

The hunt for the glasses was accompanied by the ringing

of the vicarage doorbell – an irritating interruption, as far as Minerva was concerned – which David answered, checking in at the hall mirror on the way. Minerva strained to hear who the untimely visitor might be, and was bemused when the cool, calm and collected vicar returned with an excited looking Isis in tow.

'Isis, what brings you here?' said Minerva, smoothing down her top.

'Minerva, I had to tell someone,' said Isis, waving an envelope towards the angels on the ceiling. 'And I thought you might be here.'

Minerva couldn't be sure whether Isis was looking embarrassed because she knew what they'd been up to, or because of something else entirely. Isis was a complex mixture of emotions, most of which she had little control over and Minerva had little tolerance for. They shared much, in some very odd ways.

'What is it, then?' Minerva pointed to the envelope, fluttering around at the end of Isis' fingers.

'Do you remember that competition I entered last year?'

'No, I don't. Please remind me.'

'Shall I put the kettle on?' asked David. 'Do sit down, Isis, and I'll bring some refreshments,' he said, pointing to the sofa.

Isis seemed to take forever to settle down on the sofa. Perhaps the scattered cushions on the floor had something to do with it – and if not, then the curled-up purple knickers squashed into the corner certainly did. If Minerva hadn't appeared so blatantly blasé, Isis would have had no option but to leave, but her news was far too important to flippantly discard for a pair of flippantly discarded knickers.

'Well?' said Minerva, sounding quite bored.

Isis shuffled from one end of the sofa to the other. 'My belly dancing magazine...*Wobbly Women*... The November edition had a competition and I entered it... Do you remember?'

'I do vaguely...yes. What was it for?'

'Well,' Isis looked down at the envelope still fluttering in her hand: ' I've won a Wobbly Women's Weekend for two...on a health farm!' She could hardly contain herself.

'When is it?' said Minerva, just about managing to contain herself. 'And *who* are you thinking of taking?'

David swept into the room with a large tray balanced in the crook of one arm, and closed the door behind him with great care. *Such poise and grace*, thought Minerva.

Isis cleared her throat and looked nervously from one to the other. 'Well, I was rather hoping you would like to come with me... It might be fun...don't you think?'

'That's very kind of you, Isis,' replied Minerva politely, glancing sideways at David. 'When is it, exactly?'

'It's soon...next weekend in Dragonsbury, not too far away.' Isis raised her eyebrows. 'Are you...um...free?'

Minerva glanced at David who was pouring the coffee with great care and concentration into the cups. She reached for her handbag and pulled out her diary.

Thumbing through the already worn pages, she stopped in deep concentration before looking up at Isis. 'That's the weekend of Imbolc, actually...'

'Oh...'

'...And I can't think of a better way to celebrate it than a jolly jaunt to Dragonsbury, of all places... I just love the energy there! Of course I'll come with you, Isis – what fun; but *health farm* did you say? How healthy and how farm-like does that mean, I wonder? I trust we won't be sharing bed space with

Ermintrude, not to mention lining up for our mung beans with a porky pig or two?'

'According to this,' Isis passed the fluttering envelope over to Minerva, 'it appears to be very…organic and rustic…Just how you like things.'

Minerva took some time to study the contents of the brochure inside the envelope and quickly handed it back to Isis.

'It doesn't appear to mention any alcohol restrictions, so that's fine with me. A bit of wobbly dancing first thing, shamanic journeying last thing and a macrobiotic menu in between sounds completely do-able don't you think? I may have to pass on the colonic irrigation session, though…nobody is sticking anything in or up my bottom, thank you very much!' She paused and turned to David. 'There's nothing particularly requiring my presence on next weekend's agenda, is there, David? You won't miss me if I toddle off with Isis for a Wobbly Weekend? It is, after all *healthy* to spend some time apart, don't you think?'

'Just the W.I. meeting on Saturday night,' smiled David. 'But I'm sure we can manage without you, Minerva…too much jam and Jerusalem doesn't mix too well with the Martell, does it?'

Was he trying to be funny? Minerva wasn't sure. Sarcasm somehow didn't sit quite right with a man of the cloth. She decided in that moment, without further deliberation, to fully indulge in the trip to Dragonsbury with Isis and wobble as much as she liked. She would answer to no man, cloth-wrapped, dog-collared or otherwise.

'That's it then, Isis, it's a date!' Minerva shot up from her chair. 'Shall we leave the vicar to the peace and quiet of a well-earned siesta? No doubt he has some important matters of the cloth to attend to,' she said, strutting out of the door.

However, catching her handbag on the door handle catapulted her back into the room where the rather dramatic exit was lost on David who was too busy gathering up the tray and its contents as Minerva rebounded towards him.

Unfortunately, Isis was caught in the cross-fire as she scrambled to join Minerva, ducking away from the upturned tray, leaving the fountain of milk and lukewarm coffee splattering over the beige carpet and down David's trouser legs. There followed a clashing of bodies, a clattering of cups and saucers and the tray rolled into its final position at the foot of the grandfather clock as it chimed the hour.

'Good lord,' said David, not quite so calm and collected. 'What happened there?'

'*That*,' said Minerva, brushing biscuit crumbs from her skirt, 'Was the three-fold law in action...'

'I could've sworn it was *you* in action, Minerva,' he quipped. 'Are we all okay?'

'You mean it all rebounded on you very quickly?' said Isis, stooping to rescue the tray and its contents.

While Minerva appreciated the explanation from Isis she was impatient to get out of the vicarage before things got any worse. It was turning into one of those days.

'Something like that, yes, Isis,' she said, looking at David. 'Do you need a hand to clear up?'

'It's fine, really,' he said, opening the door to give them a wide berth. 'You ladies have some arrangements to make I think... Oh, and don't forget these Minerva,' David handed over her tarot cards.

Did he wink at her? Nothing would surprise Minerva at the moment. She supposed he was certain to be a little cock-sure of himself, given the circumstances and the Two of Cups. It was, after all, the most romantic card in the deck and usually had that effect on people. Just as well she was going away for a few days; it would give him time to cool off. Some healthy rationing in the love department wasn't a bad thing sometimes and besides…it was never a good thing to give the impression of being too keen.

* * *

The next week passed quickly and the day of the coach trip dawned.

On a dark winter's afternoon the following Friday, they arrived at their destination among the twinkling street lights of Dragonsbury. Minerva was glad of the decision to leave Mr. Morris at home; the poor old thing would have struggled on the roads and it just wasn't worth the worry, especially with Isis in the passenger seat – she was bad enough on the coach… The constant lip-chewing and hand-wringing from Isis on the journey had almost driven Minerva mad. Sitting in such close proximity to one as highly strung for five whole hours was not the best recipe for any kind of journey, let alone a peaceful one.

'Do you think the driver knows what the speed limit is?' asked a pale looking Isis.

'Of course he does,' snapped Minerva. 'Whatever makes you think otherwise?'

It was a question she immediately regretted, as Isis proceeded to ramble on irrationally, with the most ridiculous reasons behind them, none of which made sense. Minerva had no choice but to excavate the brandy from the depths of her bag, in the hope that it would anaesthetise Isis in some way and provide some in-flight entertainment for herself. It appeared to work – for, when they reached the drop-off point, Isis had well and truly dropped off – along with her hair-piece, which very nearly stayed on the coach, much to her and the nearby passengers' dismay.

'My hair-piece!' Isis cried, clutching her head and zig-zagging back to the coach. Her brain seemed to register on some level of awareness, while short-circuiting on another, causing Minerva to laugh out loud, along with the remainder of the passengers.

The weekend, she thought, was looking up already.

* * *

'Some food, I think, would be a good idea, Isis. You look in need of *something*,' said Minerva, peering from behind the lid of her suitcase. She was carefully leafing through the layers, wishing she hadn't packed quite as much – it was only a two-day stay – but one never knew, there was always the possibility of endless possibilities when it came to the question of attire. According to Minerva, it had to be right, and one had to be prepared for every eventuality – just in case, of course.

A groan came from the bed, where Isis lay in a sprawled heap. The bright green and yellow chiffon layers gathered in lumps around her as she curled into a semi-foetal position and let out another groan, louder than the last. 'I don't think I…' she muttered.

'*Oh yes, you can!*' said Minerva, rummaging with renewed purpose and pulling out a tiny, dark bottle. She sat down next to the pathetic figure on the bed and pushed it towards her. 'Isis, sit up and sniff some of this!'

'What is it?'

'Let me present *Such a Drag* – an effective little potion, and one of my magical remedies for apathy. A few whiffs and you'll be as right as rain, I promise you!'

'Minerva,' croaked Isis, 'I'm only just getting over the last *magical remedy* of yours. Do I have to?'

'Indeed you do, if you want to show up for dinner…after the 'Warm-up Welcome Wobble' – whatever that is – in the main hall, according to this evening's agenda. I gather it's a dance of sorts, to get us in the mood.' She looked at Isis, who looked anything but in the mood. 'Oh come on, woman… Make an effort and at least try to sit up. You'll be surprised how easy it is, once you start moving.'

After a good deal of moans, groans, splashes of cold water and a few whiffs of magical remedy later, the two woman were suitably attired and ready for action… at least Minerva was. Isis was upright – which was an improvement – and, as far as Minerva was concerned, the only way *was* up.

How true this proved to be: after the initial introductions in the main hall, the thirty-odd women began to wobble to a thudding Turkish beat, while Isis turned a deathly shade of green and up came the contents of her stomach, in full view of the others. Minerva stood speechless while Isis, who was legless, collapsed in a green and yellow heap once again.

The room circled around Isis in a hazy blur of bright, fuzzy colour and noise. Sweaty hands pressed down on her shoulders, and it was only when her nose came into contact with something wet and hard that the awful realization hit her in a vague and far- off sort of way.

'Oh dear,' said a large, wobbling woman, leaning heaving breasts over Isis. 'Is she all right?'

'Does she look all right?' said Minerva, grabbing Isis by the armpits and hauling her backwards across the floor.

Bright red faces looked on aghast as a thin trail of orange slime accompanied the two women to the side of the hall. It was hard to decide which was the less attractive sight – a slithering and semi-conscious Isis, or the row of still semi-wobbling, astounded onlookers. Minerva had no time for such petty calculations and could only think about getting Isis back to their room as quickly as possible. The brandy was calling louder than any micro-robotic meal could ever do, with a bunch of contemptuous, wobbly women tutting and muttering under their breath. She would never live this down, not without the aid of an alcoholic plaster, anyway. In fact, a Saturday night of jam and Jerusalem with the W.I. glittered in bright neon lights before her and the temptation to hop on a coach back home was almost too much to ignore.

But ignore it she did, and with head held as high as she could manage while trying to cope with the dead weight of a comatose Isis, Minerva left the hall with the decorum and dignity of a true warrior woman, albeit a wobbly one. The only battle she planned to lose was with the brandy bottle, but the war, she predicted, was now on with anyone who dared raise an eyebrow or snigger in their direction with any kind of contempt for the preceding incident. As unfortunate a scene as it was, it was by no means worthy of the condemnation she felt.

Hell hath no greater fury than a Witch scorned. It was as simple as that.

* * *

Joe appeared with the first snowdrops.

Minerva said it was a sign. Of what, Ronnie didn't know, but she did allow herself the time to wonder about it. And that, in itself, was something different. Different to the dull state of limbo she had found herself in, and different to the small, grey world that smelt familiar and looked the same...every day. Different from the closed-in walls and dark shadows... A glimpse of the faintest light.

He looked awkward at first. 'Hey, Ron,' he said.

'Joe... What brings you here?'

He stood at the doorway of the living room. Unsure.

'For God's sake, come in. She won't bite!' said Ronnie, throwing a quick glance at the Small Thing sleeping in the bouncy chair, surrounded by a sea of pink and blue fairies: a baby blanket from Isis.

He walked in and sat down, his movements quick and wooden. 'Yeah, well, what with Christmas and all that...it's been kind of weird. First one without Mum and I didn't know how things were...here.' He looked at the baby and back at Ronnie.

'Well, as you can see, things have changed quite a bit,' said Ronnie, with a wry smile.

'I'm sorry about Bob.'

She got up quickly. 'Would you like a cuppa?'

He nodded and flashed a smile at her as she hurried to the kitchen.

'You look different,' he said, as she returned with two steaming mugs.

'Well, it's not surprising, is it? A lot's happened.'

'You could say that, Ron!'

He was looking at her strangely and she wasn't sure how to

take it.

'I don't like it…' she said. 'This isn't me, is it?' She searched his face for an answer.

'Well, no, it wasn't before. But it is *now*…' He nodded at the Small Thing and back to her. 'You never said you were…'

'I know. I was going to…the day it happened. I was coming to tell you after the ride…' She couldn't look at him. She fixed her gaze on the bird table outside and felt herself stiffen.

'Well, at least you have something now to take your mind off it, to keep you busy.'

'Take my mind off it? Do you really think I can forget Bob just like that? Every time I look at her, I'm reminded. Every time I hear her, I remember… Every time.' She bit her lip hard.

Joe came and sat beside her and placed his arm around her shoulder. It was a friendly gesture, she knew that. She stiffened again. They didn't say anything, only staring into space, each in their own world.

'It's all right you know, Ron,' he said, pulling her to him. 'It's all right.'

'Is it?' she asked. 'Is it really, Joe?'

He squeezed her and that's when she broke. She didn't even recognize the sound. It came from somewhere else, not her. It was deep and guttural, like a wounded animal.

He held her while the pain and memories poured out…until it had all rolled into one and consumed her totally. She needed to purge herself of it. She pressed hard into him and buried it. She wanted it gone.

The moment was brought to an abrupt end by the waking sounds of the Small Thing who began to fidget and murmur. Ronnie didn't wait for the cry, but got up instinctively to soothe her. It worked.

'What's her name?' asked Joe.

'Morrigan… Goddess of war and death.'

'Don't tell me; your mum thought of it?'

'No, I did. Appropriate, don't you think?'

She held the Small Thing up to him and he was taken aback by the shock of dark hair and the translucent skin, the smell of baby. 'Wow, Ron, she's tiny!' He held out a finger to the doll-like hand and she grasped it. 'Hey, the mighty Morrigan, eh? Sounds like a cool name to me…'

'Yeah, Mum thinks so, too. She's talking of having a naming ceremony – a wiccaning.'

'You mean like a christening?'

'Kind of, yes…a Witchy christening.'

'Are you okay with that?' He said.

'I am, yes; the whole Pagan thing feels right to me.'

'I suppose, and as she's been born into it, she might as well be branded a Witch right from the start!' He laughed.

'Guess where Mum wants to do it?'

'Well, definitely not in a church, I'd say. Somewhere outside, knowing Minerva… Let me think… the beach?'

She laughed. 'Yeah, you guessed right!'

'I like it…when?'

'Ostara…the Spring Equinox.'

He looked puzzled.

'March 21st, on the beach,' she said. 'Will you come?'

'Well, yeah…if you want me to.' He looked a little embarrassed. 'I'll be there.'

'I'd like that, Joe. It would mean a lot.' She smiled. 'You could bring your guitar!'

'Whoa there… Hang on a minute.'

'Oh Joe, please! It would be lovely….' pleaded Ronnie.

Joe pondered for a moment. 'Looks like I'll be there, then,' he said, and looked at the tiny finger still curled around his. 'You Witches have us right where you want us, don't you?'

After all that's happened, thought Ronnie, *surely that can't be a bad thing?*

12

Pearlies and Beaches

Minerva couldn't wait for the Wobbly Women Weekend to be over. From their rather wobbly arrival on the Friday night, it was one thing after another – a slippery and downward spiral of awkward and embarrassing moments – cushioned by brandy, numbed with more brandy…and leaving nothing but brandy hangovers in their wake. Minerva and Isis had had enough.

Sunday morning dawned and, battling with brandy-fuelled insomnia, the two friends took an early morning walk to the remains of the campfire where they had gathered the night before with the group of wobbly women, who'd insisted they join them for an evening of shamanic goings-on.

The two women stood with blank expressions, looking on at the tree-stump seats around the dying embers of the fire.

'Even *these* are wobbly,' said Minerva, mounting a stump in precarious fashion.

'Yes, I see what you mean,' said Isis. 'I have a rather vague recollection of you wobbling off one and almost ending up in the fire… If it hadn't been for that rather large lady, who came to your rescue...'

'Oh, and which *rather large lady* would that be, I wonder?' Sneered Minerva. 'Bless them all, Isis, but really... We're downright anorexic by comparison, don't you think? I thought I'd kissed goodbye to the skinniness of my youth *in* my youth, if you know what I mean? Until I came here, that is. I suppose that's a positive to be taken from the weekend, at least.'

'Minerva, you really can be cruel at times,' said Isis. 'If it hadn't been for that lady pulling you back from the fire, you'd have been in it or on it, and with all that brandy inside you; you would've gone up...'

'...Like a petrol bomb!' laughed Minerva. 'Now, that would've sent out a few smoke signals, hey, Ice? Something to get those jungle drums beating a little more, shall we say...energetically?' She rolled her eyes. 'Oh come on, Ice, you must admit – it was all a bit downbeat, wasn't it? I thought we were supposed to be *journeying* somewhere...you know, going down with the drum to a dark and distant place – not a slow boat to China on some funeral march!'

'Minerva, you're being ridiculous,' snapped Isis. 'I'm going in for breakfast.' She looked over towards the dining hall, where lights were flashing on in the darkness.

Minerva leaned across and pulled Isis back. 'We've one more thing to do before lining up for our bean sprout cereal...' she produced a tea-light from her pocket and placed it on one of the stumps. 'A candle for Brigid at Imbolc...for good harvests and healthy babies, especially our dear little Morrigan...to initiate a new soul into the Old Ways, under the power and protection of the Goddess... May she bright and blessed be.'

The two women watched the candle as it weaved and flickered in the cold morning air. Their thoughts turned to home and the year ahead, to babies and innocence and the return of the Goddess as she danced in the flames.

There was something else dancing and lingering in the dying remains of the fire, although Minerva was too caught up in the magical moment to notice… but Isis did.

'Good lord and lady…' said Isis, peering into the still-glowing embers. 'Are those what I think they are? Minerva…look!'

Minerva frowned as she returned from the floating ether of the magical realms. How inconvenient, to be interrupted just as one communed with the Goddess, especially at such a poignant moment. It was times like this, thought Minerva, when Isis lacked all sense of occasion.

'Where and what are you talking about Isis?' grumbled Minerva, stifling a yawn.

'Right there…' Isis pointed at something pale and almost translucent on the ground in front of them.

'Well I never…surely it isn't…? It's not, is it?' Said Minerva, as she leaned over for a better look. 'It damn well is, too!'

Wobbling forwards and reaching out, Minerva picked up the gleaming object, while Isis looked on. Clutching it in a closed fist, Minerva seemed to take great delight in slowly delivering it right up to the alarmed face of Isis and opening her fingers, more slowly still, to reveal what was in her hand. Isis was not one for surprises – as Minerva well knew – but she couldn't help herself: it was just too tempting.

'Oh, my Goddess!' Cried Isis. 'What on earth are *they* doing here?'

'Well,' said a very serious Minerva, 'One can only assume – given the evidence…' she looked closely into her hand, '…the obvious.'

Isis stared wide-eyed at Minerva. 'And what is that?'

'Like I said...it's obvious, isn't it?' She whispered: 'Somebody's died.'

'You mean somebody fell into the fire and...*died?*'

'Why else would these false teeth be there?' said Minerva. 'Always the last thing to go, you know...teeth. The final remains of the suit of clay.'

Isis gasped. 'What about the bones? Wouldn't they be here, too?'

'Perhaps we ought to look...'

'Shouldn't we call the police?'

'We need to tread very carefully, Isis. I smell a rat, don't you?' She looked quickly over her shoulder. 'I knew there was something odd about those wobbly women...bones make good carcass material...nice stews...'

'You don't mean...they're cannibals?'

It may have been a cold, February morning, but Isis had worked up a sweat and her heart was pounding through her ear drums.

Minerva signalled for silence. 'I knew all that shamanic stuff didn't feel quite right,' she said. 'All those wobbly women were doing the dance of the psychopomp – transporter of souls – heralding the arrival of *this* poor soul...' she thrust the teeth skywards, '...torn from this world and thrown prematurely into the next... Despicable!'

'Minerva, we have to get away from here. What if we're next?'

'Isis, for Goddess' sake, calm down,' said Minerva. 'And what's with all this hand wringing? You never used to do that! First, we must conduct our own burial protection spell for this dear soul,' she said, getting up. 'Round the circle, three times three,' she began to walk sun-wise, holding her palms aloft, 'Love and truth will set you free... Protect this sacred soul's journey... Goddess bless, so mote it be!'

Isis joined her and they walked together in solemn procession three times around, chanting the spell over the top of the false teeth in Minerva's outstretched hands. It was a touching sight as well as a peculiar one, and certainly not the kind of ceremony either of them had anticipated having to carry out, given the time and place, but – as every wise woman knows – one must be prepared to heed the call of magic, whenever the moment presents itself.

Spontaneity is a Witch's best friend.

No sooner had they finished the ritual and escorted the poor soul on its final journey, they realized that – apart from the teeth – they had company.

A somewhat sheepish figure circled the remains of the fire; head down and with hands thrust deeply into her pockets. Minerva recognized her as one of the wobbly women and, stuffing the teeth quickly into her own pocket, bid her good morning. There was no response from the wobbly woman at all. Not one to be ignored, Minerva repeated herself. This time, a low mumble emerged from the figure.

'Is it breakfast time yet?' prompted Minerva. 'I'm feeling quite peckish, now that we've finished our morning walk!'

Isis thought the woman looked a bit lost; in fact, she could almost be looking for something... 'Can we help in any way?' she said.

The woman continued to shuffle around the fire and, with a shrug of resignation, looked up to reveal a jolly sort of face and a very toothless smile. Minerva leapt into immediate action and, with a subtle sleight of hand, managed to take the teeth from her pocket and return them to the fire. Isis was quick to follow her lead and proceeded to surprise no-one more than herself with a hint of the early morning drama queen.

'Oh, look!' she said, picking up the dentures and handing them over. 'Are these what you're looking for?'

With a swift brush of her coat sleeve and a sharp blow across the false teeth, the wobbly woman popped them straight into her mouth.

'Now, that's better!' she beamed. 'Thanks very much, me dears… Breakfast will be a lot easier now with me pearlies back in. Must've been all that dancing about last night… What with the drums and bums and tums… I was wobbling all over and they fell out, so they did!' Her Devonshire accent rang in the cold air. 'Funny how you don't really appreciate what you've got until it's gone, don't you think?'

Before they had a chance to answer her, she'd made a sharp exit left, towards the dining hall.

'Did that really happen or did I dream it all?' asked Minerva, with a glazed expression.

'Good question,' said an equally baffled Isis. 'But not worth spending too much time over… We have better things to do.'

'Yes,' said Minerva, 'like going home, for one, and a good English fry-up for another… One can only take so much of this healthy life, Isis: everything in moderation, after all.'

* * *

The days leading up to the Spring Equinox were filled with the tingle of new life, something that had been missing for far too long. It crept back with the longer days and the warm air. It tiptoed in crocus-bright footsteps around Crafty Cottage and it chirruped in the bushes and trees. It nodded in the heads of daffodils; it pushed out in swollen buds and squeezed up slowly from the earth.

Mother Nature was revving up…and so was Minerva.

She could hardly contain her excitement. She was high priestess at her own granddaughter's wiccaning. How wonderful! She could think of nothing better to highlight and celebrate this time of life for all of them. It was going to be a magical affair and in the perfect location…on a beach! It was just how it should be: honouring the Goddess and the God, the earth mother and her consort. One could not wish for a more idyllic setting on such an occasion.

Finalizing the details with Isis was the last job before the big day.

'Where's the list, Minerva?'

'I thought you had it, Isis,' said Minerva, between sips of brandy – a celebratory mid-morning nip had been far too tempting. 'You had it, I'm sure, when we were going over things last week.'

Isis delved into her bag and out again. 'It's definitely not in here.'

'Are you sure?' asked Minerva. 'Where did you have it last?'

If there was one thing that irritated Isis (apart from misplaced assumptions: she was sure she didn't have the list), it was stupid questions. Maybe the brandy could have waited until later. 'I'm sure *you* had it, Minerva; you were writing it on the back of an envelope… Why would I take it home?'

And if there was one thing that irritated Minerva, it was being accused (wrongly, of course) of losing something she didn't have in the first place – followed by a stupid question. She pulled a face. 'Oh, look, if it was all on the back of an envelope, surely it can't be too much to remember, can it? I distinctly wanted to keep it as simple as possible. As long as we have the altar tools, the readings, the paper cups and the alcohol…naturally.'

'And the baby?'

Minerva smiled, 'Ah yes, dear little Morrigan…such a sweetie. I'm sure it'll all be fine, Ice.'

'Is David coming?'

'He wouldn't miss it for the world… But obviously he'll be taking a back seat in the readings department on the day. He is, however, bringing his guitar, as I thought some musical accompaniment might be nice, don't you?'

'Isn't Joe coming?' asked Isis.

'Yes, I believe so. I'm so pleased for Ronnie.'

'I'm sure I heard Ronnie saying he was bringing his guitar.'

'Ah! That won't be a problem, will it? Surely they can do something together, can't they?'

'I have no idea,' said Isis. 'I suppose it depends on what songs they know, doesn't it?'

'What do you mean, *what they know*?' said Minerva. 'Don't most guitarists know most of the same songs? Isn't that how it works?'

'Are we all going together?'

'I think that'll be nice, don't you?'

'Yes, whatever you say…' said Isis, reaching for the brandy. 'I'm sure it'll all work out just fine.'

* * *

Ronnie was feeling better. She felt a buoyancy that had been absent for longer than she could remember. It seemed to return when Joe did, and for that, she was grateful. Spring was in the air, in her step and, according to her mother, in the Equinox.

Everything was arranged. They were driving down in convoy to the beach, which was just a couple of miles down the road. David was bringing Isis, and Sophia and Joe were coming in Sophia's car, while Minerva, Ronnie and baby Morrigan were taking Mr. Morris.

Minerva had insisted that Morrigan must be transported on such a momentous day in Mr. Morris, as his days were numbered. She'd bought a special, leather bound photo album to mark the occasion and titled it, 'Magical Morris Memories', with sticky silver labels. Nostalgia, as far as Minerva was concerned, was best displayed in photo form.

After the usual 'Operation Load-up Mr. Morris' was over and the reluctant engine chanted at in the usual manner, they were off.

'Isn't this just wonderful, Ronnie? Morris, maiden, mother and crone all off to a wiccaning on our lovely beach!'

'Yes, Mum, it's great,' said Ronnie, attempting to fit some mittens onto Morrigan's tiny hands. 'Thanks for organizing it all.'

'Oh, I've enjoyed every minute,' said Minerva, checking her headdress in the mirror. Sprigs of hawthorn and ivy jutted out at various angles, digging into the low ceiling. She liked to be as authentic as possible; one couldn't put a price on the real thing. She only hoped it would last until after the ceremony before it drooped miserably.

'While I think about it, darling, is Joe bringing his guitar?'

'Yes, why?'

'Oh, David's bringing his and...'

'Mum!'

'What's the problem?'

'Well, they're completely different people, aren't they? And

178

isn't that reflected in what they play?' Ronnie pondered for a moment. 'Oh, I suppose it'll be all right... It might be quite good having a contrast. Anyway, I can't see a battle of egos on the cards, can you?'

'Not a bit of it.' Said Minerva with quiet confidence. 'I checked beforehand: Temperance followed by the Three of Cups. Harmonic celebrations all round... It doesn't get any better than that, Ron!'

They arrived in the car park to find the others assembling, with David and Joe huddled over their instruments in deep discussion. Ronnie breathed a sigh of relief and by the time they had extracted themselves from the Morris, an air of growing excitement filled the air.

Minerva bent down over the boot of the old car to gather her equipment and everyone was handed something to carry – with the exception of Ronnie, who was carrying Morrigan – and they began the trek along the old Roman road to the beach.

'Has anyone got a lighter or matches?' Asked Minerva, suddenly thinking of candles and fires. A ceremony without either didn't bear thinking about.

'Yes, Miss!' Joe put up his hand and caught Ronnie's smile.

'Good,' said Minerva, 'I knew I'd forget something.'

'What about the altar tools and the readings?' Isis called from the rear.

Minerva nodded. 'Brandy? Paper cups?'

'Brandy...yes,' said Minerva, 'but damn, I've forgotten the bloody cups!'

David shot her a look of mock disdain.

'Sorry!' She said. 'We're just going to have to rough it, folks!'

'Since it's only you and I that drink the stuff, I think we'll manage,' said Isis, flapping along in full costume and sandals, hair-piece half on and half off. The late March wind was not being kind to her.

By the time they got to the beach, the wind had whipped itself up into a frenzy, making all civilized means of communication impossible. They resorted to shouting at each other, which caused a great deal of confusion and, when dark clouds appeared from the west, Minerva was fast giving up hope of any kind of ceremony, let alone a decent one.

'Damn you, elements!' she raged at the sky, signalling to Isis for the brandy.

'Is there no shelter at all?' Screamed Sophia.

'We could go in the chapel.' David's dulcet tones could just about be heard above the wind.

All eyes fell on him.

'I'm sure it'll be fine… Come on, everyone.'

How very God-like, thought Minerva, as she gave the brandy back to Isis and followed David's lead to the seventh-century chapel. Could he actually be the new Messiah?

The small, simple building had a deeply spiritual essence, a palpable energy which filtered out from the stone walls, touching the soul of anyone who entered.

'This is just perfect,' said Minerva, as David shut the great wooden door behind them. 'Are you sure it's all right to carry on?'

'Please do,' said David, taking his guitar out of its case.

Joe followed suit and they sat together and tuned their instruments while the others organized themselves. Ronnie and Sophia fussed over Morrigan, who was completely calm and unaffected by the whole ordeal.

'She's being so good, Ron, bless her.' Sophia touched her tiny head.

'I know; she's a little angel, really…' said Ronnie. 'Don't know about a warrior Witch, though!'

'She's got plenty of time yet,' laughed Sophia.

David and Joe found they had a number of tunes in common and proceeded to work out a set for the ceremony.

'Nice guitar, Joe; I have a soft spot for Yamaha's myself,' said David, as he settled on to one of the cold wooden benches and began to play.

'I bow to the infinite wisdom of the god Yamaha,' smiled Joe. 'Written all my songs on this…' He patted the guitar's slim neck. 'It's my old faithful.'

The harsh, bracing effects of the noisy elements remained outside and they were left to the peace and stillness of the small, humble building as it tranquilized them all, none more so than Minerva. In appearance she was far from tranquil looking, but, for all her windswept witchy and wild woman ways, it must be said she radiated something that did not look out of place in a house of God.

Isis glimmered and shimmered in rainbow chiffon and sparkling gold sandals…emanating an air of the exotic and slightly wonky. The wind, in its temper, had brutally groomed her hair into a lop-sided perfection piece to her head where it clung for dear life.

But none of it mattered.

The ceremony was a glimpse of pure magic in the midst of all the madness. It was a moment in time remaining long enough for them all to savour the taste of that magic, and realize that it was the flip-side of the very same coin. Seldom is there one without the other.

Afterwards, as they fussed around baby Morrigan, Ronnie slipped outside to find Joe.

'Guitar sounded great, Joe,' she said.

'Thanks. The acoustics in there are fantastic, aren't they?'

'Thank you for being here; it means a lot to me.'

'Really?' said Joe.

'Yes…really,' smiled Ronnie.

'I'm glad about that, Ron.'

He was going to kiss her, she was almost certain of it. But the creak of the chapel door and the appearance of the others stopped him. Pouring out one by one they huddled together against the raging wind and cold.

'Everyone back to Crafty Cottage for cakes and ale!' cried Minerva. 'Or bread and brandy…music and merriment… whatever takes your fancy!'

'No, you mean whatever takes *your* fancy, Minerva!' laughed David.

'Well, what's life without a bit of what you fancy?' said Minerva, slipping an arm through his and pulling him towards her. 'Don't you agree, vicar?'

THE END

Afterword

I hope you enjoyed the story as much as I loved writing it… and if you have a couple of minutes to leave a review on Amazon it will be greatly appreciated.

Book 2 - Bonkers and Broomsticks - releases May 2019.

'Minerva's mission to find her missing sex drive is rudely interrupted when her mother comes to stay at Crafty Cottage. While daughter Ronnie is discovering her psychic gifts and the spirit world, Minerva finds a world with her mother in it, unbearable. Can she manage to hang onto her sanity with woodland spells, brandy and the heaven sent David by her side or will those murderous tendencies get the better of her?'

For news, updates on future books and a free copy of the prequel - Black Dogs and Broomsticks - sign up for the Treehouse Magic newsletter.
www.sheenacundy.com

About the Author

Songwriter. Storyteller. Sheena Cundy is a teacher of horse and rider, reader of the Tarot and Reiki Master.

Her love of horses, the healing and magical arts since childhood has never waned and continues to fascinate and filter into her writing any which way it can.

The Madness and the Magic is the debut novel she wrote to keep out of prison, a straitjacket and the divorce courts while battling with murderous tendencies and all kinds of hormonal horrors during a mid-life crisis.

Apart from Witch Lit and other magical fiction, she also writes spiritual non-fiction and sings and writes the songs for her pagan band, Morrigans Path.

You can connect with me on:

- 🌐 https://sheenacundy.com
- 🐦 https://twitter.com/OrgSheena
- 📘 https://www.facebook.com/sheena.cundywriter
- 🔗 https://morriganspath.bandcamp.com
- 🔗 https://www.instagram.com/treehouse_witch

Subscribe to my newsletter:

- ✉ https://www.subscribepage.com/blackdogs

Printed in Great Britain
by Amazon

37855480R00111